Last Hanging at Paradise Meadow

G·K
Hall
&Cº

Also published in Large Print
from G.K. Hall by Stephen Bly:

Hard Winter at Broken Arrow Crossing
False Claims at the Little Stephen Mine

This Large Print Book carries the
Seal of Approval of N.A.V.H.

Last Hanging at Paradise Meadow

Stephen Bly

G.K. Hall & Co.
Thorndike, Maine

Published in 1995 by arrangement with Crossway Books, a division of Good News Publishers.

G.K. Hall Large Print Western Collection.

The text of this Large Print edition is unabridged.
Other aspects of the book may vary from the original edition.

Set in 16 pt. News Plantin by Warren Doersam.

Printed in the United States on permanent paper.

Library of Congress Cataloging in Publication Data

Bly, Stephen A., 1944–
    Last hanging at Paradise Meadow / Stephen Bly.
      p.   cm.
    ISBN 0-7838-1249-3 (lg. print : hc)
    1. Large type books. I. Title.
  [PS3552.L93L37 1995]
  813'.54—dc20
                                    95-3702

For
DAVE and DENISE,
tickled
pink

ONE

I never could do this!" Brannon fumed to himself as he stared into the mirror.
"Couldn't I just wear a bandana? Oh, no, that wasn't good enough for Miss Velvet Wendell! 'You simply must wear a tie,' she pouted. Look at that! Half of it hanging down like a horse's tail, and the other looks like it was a flag blowin' in the breeze! Stiff shirt . . . clean fingernails — why do weddings have to be so perfect, anyway?"

Stuart Brannon stomped back across his bedroom at the Davis & Wendell Hotel. The twelve-foot by twelve-foot quarters with a window on the main street of Tres Casas, New Mexico Territory, had been his home for over five months. His spurs jingled, and his boot heels banged as he paced around the room.

"Spurs?" he muttered. "She didn't say anything about spurs. Well, Miss Wendell," he addressed the mirror once more, "I'm wearing spurs to the wedding, and that's that!"

He wiped a smudge off the mirror with his white linen shirt sleeve and stared closer at the image.

A man turns thirty, and suddenly there's gray hair at the temples. It's these cold winters, that's what it is. I ought to be down in that Arizona sun! I don't belong up here!

Brannon picked up the Chinese silk vest with rounded notched lapels and embroidered gold design. He fumbled with the brass buttons.

Only faro dealers and tonic salesmen would wear something like this on purpose.

He gave a yank at the cinch at the back of the vest and drew it up so tight that the buttons puckered.

"Now look at this!" he groaned. "How do you loosen one of these?" Adjusting the vest, he pulled on the new wool suit coat.

At least the coat fits, and the sleeves are long enough. Course I'll have to wear my gun high and keep it on the left side until I reach the church.

He had promised Velvet that he would not walk down the aisle with a Colt on his hip.

Finally, he lifted the brand-new beaver felt wide-brimmed hat that had been lying crown down on the dresser. He slipped his old, sweaty horsehair hatband over the hat and then placed it on his head.

"This is the silliest thing I ever heard of," he complained. "The hat that I bought up at Conchita isn't even broke in yet, and she insists I wear a new hat. Then she tells me I can't even wear it in the church building. This isn't Boston or San Francisco. It's not even Denver or Virginia City!"

Brannon took one more look at himself in the mirror. Then he took a gold locket off the dresser and slipped it into his vest pocket. Instantly, he pulled the locket back out. He flipped it open and glanced down at Lisa's picture.

"Well, darlin', here I am with white shirt, clean fingernails, and slicked-down hair. I haven't felt this uncomfortable since the day you and I got married. I never counted on needing to spruce up like this again." He jammed the locket back in his vest and then picked up the badge off the dresser.

"I'm still sheriff of Tres Casas. At least until Monday morning, and no sweet-talking lady is going to keep me from wearin' this badge."

Brannon barged downstairs and found the lobby of the hotel, which also doubled as a dining room, mostly vacant. Normally there would have been a late Saturday afternoon crowd, but the big wedding of two of the town's prominent citizens had emptied most businesses and filled the church to overflowing.

Tres Casas had never really seemed like home to Brannon. Now, as he stepped out on the wooden sidewalk, he felt again that sense of unease. Tucked up in the hills of northern New Mexico near the Colorado border, Tres Casas was a town trying to decide if it wanted to be a sleepy Spanish village or a rip-roaring mining supply camp. Brannon didn't know the answer, but he knew it was time for him to change the direction of his life. The wedding would mark the end — and the beginning.

April rains still puddled the main street, and

Brannon chose his steps carefully as he crossed it and turned towards the church. Without thinking he pulled out his pocket watch and glanced at the time.

Suddenly he stopped and flipped open the watch again.

"3:00?" he mumbled. "It can't still be —"

"Sheriff!"

He turned to see Harvey Lloyd Sanger and his wife Loretta scurry to his side.

"Sheriff," Loretta scolded, "it's 3:30 P.M.! You'll have Velvet worried sick if you don't get down to the church!"

"Yes, ma'am, 3:30 you say? I guess my watch stopped. Tell her I'm on my way. I'll just check on the jail." He tipped his hat to Mrs. Sanger.

"Well," she added, "they can't get started without you!"

Brannon reset his watch and glanced up and down the street as he passed in front of the Mercantile.

By nightfall this town will be crowded with cowboys, miners, and drifters. This wedding will be nothing but a memory.

He could see up the street the crowd of buggies, people, and horses around the church.

We haven't had this much excitement since that politician passed out free watermelons.

Brannon pushed the unlocked office door open with his right boot and glanced across the darkened room towards the two jail cells.

"Keo? Keo! Is that you in there!" he shouted

10

at the older man roped and gagged in the first cell.

He stomped over to the iron gate, fumbled to open it with his key, and then knelt down to untie his part-time deputy, Keo Thane.

"They snuck up on me, Stuart, they did. Two of them. Thar's two of 'em. One short and skinny, the other maybe a Mexican, you know, sort of dark? They pulled Skinner and Eureka out of the cell, tied me up, and then ran out the back door like they was being chased!"

"How long ago?" Brannon finished untying his deputy's feet.

"Not more than ten minutes, I expect," Keo reported.

"Why would anyone want to bust out Skinner and Eureka? They were only in here until to-morrow anyway."

"What do you want me to do?" Keo asked. "Shall I go get Fletcher?"

Brannon tugged at his tie and stepped back out into the office. "No, no, he's down at the church already. I'm sure they've already drifted out of town. They're not worth following. Busting the mirror at the Lavender Slipper isn't cause to form a posse over."

He pushed his hat to the back of his head. "Listen, scoot down to the church and tell Fletcher what happened. I'm going to make one round to see that everything's quiet. I'll be there before four o'clock. Weddings never start on time anyway. Tell Fletcher to calm the bride down.

11

That's what a best man is supposed to do, isn't it?"

"You're the one in the wedding, not me." Keo laughed. "Do you mind if I just stay down there and watch the proceedings myself? It ain't ever' day that the sheriff of Tres Casas goes parading around all slicked up like that."

"That's fine. I'll be right there." Brannon unlocked the gun case and grabbed his Winchester.

I'm not going to carry a rifle to the wedding!

He replaced the gun, turned on his heel, and left the office.

"That's the trouble with this job." Brannon gazed at the street once more. "There's never any time off."

He walked quickly to the corner and turned down Trotter's Gulch Road. One by one he pushed open the front doors and gazed into the dark, smoke-filled saloons and gaming rooms. Most were quiet, almost empty.

Just waiting until dark to really break loose.

He crossed the street, this time having little regard for the mud that now clung to his boots.

The Cat's Claw had only one chuck-a-luck game going.

At Jim Boy's a sleepy poker game yawned away in the corner.

The girls at Paris Pierre's hung laundry from the balcony.

O'Neil's Cowboy Tavern's bartender slept out front.

Brannon decided to check the Lavender Slipper

12

and then go to the wedding. He glanced at his watch. It was 3:40.

Before he shoved the door open, the declining sunlight bounced off one of the horses tied in front, and he turned to see what was causing the reflection. It was a series of silver conchos laced to the skirts of a high-horned, deep-seated, hand-carved leather saddle.

That is a nice piece of work, Brannon mused. *High silver horn? Long engraved tapaderas? Sixty-foot maguey coiled — Mexican? Keo said one was a Mexican!*

It was then that he noticed the four horses were tied to the rail rather loosely.

"Well, fella, looks like someone is planning on a quick exit," he said to the paint stallion sporting the fancy saddle.

If I bust in the back door, they'll run out here and ride off, so I guess that means barging right in.

Stepping lightly across the worn wooden sidewalk, Brannon placed his hand on the door handle.

I should have left the spurs in my room!

Quietly he cracked the door and slid inside.

The Lavender Slipper was hot, stuffy, smoky, and dark. Three men stood at the long, carved wooden bar. The one in the middle was waving his arms while telling a story. The man on his right glanced up and saw Brannon.

"Why, there's the sheriff! Come on over here, Brannon; we'll buy you a drink!" he called.

"Eureka," Brannon replied as he slipped his

13

hand up to grip the handle of his pistol, "now why did you and Skinner want to leave home without telling Daddy good-bye?"

Skinner, who had been telling the story, turned to face Brannon.

"Well, you see, Sheriff, we thought for sure you'd be down at the weddin'."

"Don't he look fine, all slicked up like that," Eureka chided.

"Purty enough to be a New York lawyer." Skinner nodded. "Well, we just didn't want to interfere with the wedding, so we decided just to let ourselves out and cause you no more concern."

"That's right, Sheriff." Eureka continued to talk but moved slowly away from the others. "These friends come by for a visit, and we just didn't think it was hospitable to let them pass through town without buying 'em a drink."

Skinner, with eyes scanning the room, moved down the bar a couple of steps. "Yes, sir, we stopped by here to pay back LaVerne for busting up his mirror."

"But," Eureka added, "LaVerne closed shop and went down there to the wedding, too, so we're just pirooting away the time, waiting for his return."

"Where's the Mexican?" Brannon asked.

"Who?" Skinner quizzed.

"The Mexican who helped you escape!" Brannon demanded.

"Surely you don't think we needed help to go set down old Keo, do ya?" Eureka drawled.

14

"I think you two would need help walking up a flight of stairs," Brannon growled. "Now, where's the Mexican that owns that flashy outfit hitched to the rail?"

Without a sound, Brannon felt a knife blade press against the back of his new suit coat.

"Leave the pistol in the holster, Señor," the voice instructed. "You like my horse?"

"I like the saddle better." Brannon didn't move. "Put down that pig sticker, or I'll have to mail that saddle to your next of kin."

"Don't threaten me. I can run this blade clear through you," he hissed.

"Well, you better do a good job of it. The last man to stick me back there got eaten by the buzzards on the Arizona desert."

"You do not know who you are talking to, Señor."

"Well, you're definitely not the ghost of Joaquin Murieta," Brannon upbraided. Then he slammed his left elbow straight back into what he hoped to be the pit of the man's stomach.

Unless he's left-handed!

He wasn't.

On impact the startled man jerked his hands up, raking the tip of the knife along Brannon's back. He heard his new suit coat and shirt rip and felt the blade scratch into his skin. Still in motion, Brannon whipped around and hammered through the black, flat-brimmed hat with the barrel of his pistol. The man crumpled to the floor, dropping a thin-bladed, bloody-tipped knife.

Before he could turn around, a whiskey bottle crashed across his wrist causing him to drop the pistol, and a chair caught him at the back of the knees, tumbling him to the floor.

Skinner kicked at his head, but Brannon caught the boot and twisted it violently, bringing him to the floor. Brannon rolled over to his knees, then dove under a table just as another chair crashed to the floor where he'd been.

He struggled to his feet in time to see the three men charge towards him. Jumping on a chair, Brannon dove for the men, bringing two crashing to the ground with him. Then he rolled over on Skinner and cracked his fist into the man's jaw twice before he took a bruising blow to the back of the head and felt glass fragments mixed with whiskey flowing down the back of his shirt.

The shorter man began kicking him in the ribs. Brannon rolled halfway across the room, escaped the blows, and regained his stance. Blood and sweat and whiskey trickled down his forehead and began to blur his vision. He jerked his tie from his neck.

Spread apart, the men approached Brannon.

"That did it," Brannon growled. "I'm tired of being nice." He surprised them by diving right into them and violently grabbed Eureka by the lapel on his coat. Brannon swung him around twice before the others could get close and slammed him, head first, into a twelve-by-twelve rough-sawn post that supported the middle of the long narrow room. Eureka crumpled to the floor and didn't move.

Skinner caught Brannon with a wild roundhouse right hook, and the little man leaped on Brannon's back, allowing Skinner to land several hard punches to the midsection. Staggering back with the weight of the little man on his shoulders, Brannon shoved him up against the wood stove that sat against the wall.

He was hoping that it would have a hot fire. It didn't.

But the impact against the cast iron and the stovepipe caused the man to lose grip and tumble, headfirst behind the stove. The man's flailing legs kicked the stovepipes loose, spraying Brannon and Skinner with soot.

Seizing the moment, Brannon plunged into Skinner with a powerful left jab, right jab, left jab, right jab. Scrambling back to avoid the punches, Skinner tripped over Eureka. Brannon's knee caught the man right under the chin, and he fell to his back gasping for breath.

By now the shorter man had pulled himself free from the stove, and Brannon could see the Mexican wiping blood from his forehead as he struggled to his feet.

"Leave the knife lay!" Brannon shouted.

"You are a dead man, Señor!" he hissed. "I am Ramon Fuente-Delgado. My father happens to be the Vice-General in Monterrey!"

"And my Father is the King of Kings in Heaven," Brannon warned. "You pick up that knife again and you'll see my Father long before you'll ever see yours." Brannon tried to smear some of the soot, whiskey, and blood from his face by rubbing his suit sleeve across his face.

"Your bluff is weak without a weapon in your hand," Fuente-Delgado panted.

"It's not a bluff," Brannon insisted.

"Neither is this, Sheriff!"

Brannon glanced out of the corner of his eye to see the short man holding a gun on him from across the room.

"Well, well," Fuente-Delgado said smirking. "Look who's going to visit El Señor. Shoot him, Dade."

"No, Dade won't shoot me." Brannon's eyes searched the floor for his dropped pistol as he stalled. "And I'll tell you why. Dade, did you ever know a man who shot an unarmed sheriff in the back and lived to talk about it?"

"What difference does that make?" Fuente shouted. "Shoot him."

"Now, maybe we act differently on this side of the border," he continued, spotting his pistol and inching his way in that direction. "You gun down an unarmed sheriff, and every lawman and posse and vigilante committee in the West will hunt you and shoot you on the spot. There's no trial . . . no jury . . . no jail time . . . no burial . . . no notifying next of kin. Oh, sure any old boy can get a little stewed and throw a punch at a sheriff. You wake up the next day in the juzgado, make your apologies, then ride on back to the ranch. Everyone's done that. But

18

shootin' in the back? That's like committing suicide."

"Shoot him!" Fuente-Delgado shouted.

"I ain't no sheriff shooter," Dade muttered. "Get them boys up and let's just ride out of here!"

A gagging cough and gasp from Skinner caused Dade to glance down at the man struggling to his knees, trying to breathe.

That was the chance Brannon wanted. He dove to the floor, grabbed his pistol, and rolled to the bar pointing his gun at Dade, who had bent down to help Skinner to his feet.

Ramon Fuente-Delgado stooped to grab his knife, but Brannon's shot separated the handle from the blade and spun both pieces across the floor.

"Skinner's choking to death, Sheriff . . . do something!" Dade pleaded. "He's done turned blue!"

"Pull his tongue out," Brannon barked.

"What?"

"You heard me, reach into his mouth and pull up his tongue. He's swallowed it."

"You mean it?" Dade asked again.

"Pull it out or he'll die." Brannon motioned with the pistol for Fuente-Delgado to join the others over by the wood stove. Grabbing a bottle off the bar, he walked over to where Eureka lay passed out by the big beam. Pulling the cork with his teeth and keeping the gun pointed at the threesome, he emptied the contents of the bottle on Eureka, who struggled to his feet, clutching his head.

Skinner started to regain some color and his breath came back to him, but he couldn't speak.

"Now, I figure you boys owe the Lavender Slipper a few dollars for damages, so just put your pokes on the table there."

"We ain't got no money, Sheriff," Dade insisted.

"Well, I think you're lying." He cocked the hammer back on the Colt. "Put your pokes on the table!"

Dade and Skinner reached into their coat pockets and tossed small leather bags onto the table.

"It's your turn, Eureka," Brannon motioned.

"I ain't got none."

"Pull off those boots!" Brannon fired a shot into the floor near Eureka, who immediately jumped back and began pulling off his boots. A small leather pouch fell to the floor.

"Well, isn't that amazing," Brannon chided, "you're richer than you thought. Leave those boots off!"

"All right, Señor Fuente-Delgado, Jr., pull the boots."

He yanked his boots off but said nothing. There was no pouch.

"Now, undo that red sash that holds up your britches," Brannon ordered him.

"You can't —"

Before Fuente finished the line, Brannon fired a bullet that whizzed between the man's legs and slammed into the wall behind him.

"You only got three shots left," Fuente-Delgado hissed, "and there are four of us."

"That's true." Brannon nodded. "One of you will live, and the other three will be dead. Only you don't know which three I will select, do you? Pull off that sash!"

"Do what he says, Ramon," Dade motioned.

Releasing the sash caused the britches to drop to the floor. His white long johns were the only clothing on the lower part of his body.

"Why, look there." Brannon motioned. "A poke tumbled out of that sash."

"You going to put us back in the jail?" Eureka asked.

"Nope. This is a wedding day, and I feel generous. I want you boys to walk out that front door. I want you to get on those horses. And I want you to ride south until you can't even remember where Tres Casas is . . . do you understand?"

"You going to let us ride off?" Dade asked.

"Yep."

"He'll shoot us in the back and say we were escaping," Fuente-Delgado raged.

"Nope." Eureka rubbed his head. "Not Brannon. We'll ride, Sheriff. Let me pull on my boots."

"Leave the boots!"

"But —" Eureka protested.

"You tried to hold back, Eureka. That'll cost you extra. Now move slowly to the door."

"Not without my trousers," Fuente-Delgado shouted.

"Oh, yeah? You'll do it. Might be a little embarrassing, but you'll do it. When you get to Monterrey, I'm sure your daddy will buy you another pair."

"I can't —" Fuente-Delgado started to protest. It was Dade and Skinner who shoved him out the door. A crowd had gathered on the sidewalk in front of the Lavender Slipper. Most hooted and hollered insults as the men sheepishly made their exit. They mounted quickly and raced their horses down Trotter's Gulch Road.

"Sheriff, how come you ain't at that weddin'?" someone called out.

Brannon holstered his pistol and glanced at his watch.

4:15!

He tried running, but the whiskey and sweat running into the cut on his back only increased the pain. He settled for a fast walk, cutting down the alley to the back of the church.

Edwin Fletcher was pacing by the back door.

"My word, Brannon, is that you under all that!" he shouted.

"Am I late? I mean, I know I'm late . . . just tell Velvet I'm here now."

"You're here? Just what part of you is here? You're covered with soot, you smell to high heaven, and your head's busted. Good grief, Brannon, your back! You've got a cut straight across your back! What happened?"

"Bring Velvet out here so I can apologize. I'll tell you about this later."

Brannon was bent over a horse trough when Velvet Wendell, holding up the train of her white wedding dress, burst through the back door.

"Well, if it isn't the sheriff! I'm so glad you decided to attend!" she fumed.

Edwin Fletcher stepped to the back door and watched.

"Look, Vel —"

"Don't 'look, Vel' me. Look at you! You looked better covered with mud up at the mine!"

"Well, there was a little trouble on the way to the church," Brannon began.

"A little trouble? A little trouble! Stuart, every day of your life is a little trouble! You thrive on it! You can't survive without it! Just one day, that's all I wanted, just one calm normal day to get married! Is that so much to ask?"

"I'm sorry, Vel . . . sincerely sorry. But you knew I was this way. I mean, look, if you have some second thoughts about me going through with this, just say so."

Without warning, Wendell let her dress fall to the ground, and she broke out in uncontrollable laughter.

Brannon looked at her and then at Fletcher who just shrugged.

Catching her breath, she shook her head. "Look at you! You are the worst-smelling, dirtiest, bloodiest man who ever, ever, ever walked down a church aisle. The Reverend will have to charge

23

you for getting blood stains cleaned off the rug. But you know what, Brannon? You know what?" She began to laugh again. "This is exactly what I expected."

"The suit did look nice." He tried to smile.

"I presume at one time you had a tie?"

"The tie? Where did that thing go?"

"And the shirt was white, correct?"

"Sure . . . and —"

"I suppose that black stuff all over your hair and coat was not intentional?"

"The stovepipe broke."

"Do you need the doc to patch up your back?"

"It's just a scrape."

She shook her head. "It's a bloody mess!"

The minister came to the back door. "Sheriff Brannon!" He shuddered. "Are you able to carry on?"

"Eh, listen, Reverend. Do you happen to have another jacket I can borrow? I sort of ruined this one."

"Well, certainly, yes, of course . . . not the same size, naturally, but nonetheless . . . I mean, we must get this service started."

Brannon couldn't get all the blood and soot off his face and hair, but he slipped on the pastor's coat and noted that the sleeves were three inches short and the top button wouldn't stretch across his chest.

"It's time to begin," the minister insisted. "I'll have them light the candles."

"The gun, Stuart, you're still packing the re-

24

volver," Fletcher cautioned.

"Leave it," Velvet said. "I've never seen him without a gun of some sort. No reason for today to be different."

"Wait," Brannon called. He sprinted over to his ripped suit coat lying on the back step of the church.

"Get back here, Brannon," Velvet growled.

"Not without the badge." He unfastened the sheriff's badge and put it on the ill-fitting coat.

"Come on, the organ's playing," she called. They scooted around to the front door of the church, where many people were standing, peering in.

"Are you sure you're not too embarrassed to go through with this?"

"Embarrassed?" She smiled. "Stuart, there isn't a man on the face of this earth I'd rather have by my side. Are you embarrassed?"

Brannon started to reach up and nervously adjust his tie, then realized that he didn't have one. "Me? I'm just as proud as a heifer who's dropped her first calf."

"I'll take that for a compliment. I'm nervous. I think it's about time for us to go down the aisle." They climbed the steps and waited for the woman at the curtain to signal them.

"Are you nervous, Stuart?" Velvet whispered.

"Not really nervous . . . just a little lonesome." He nodded.

"For Lisa?"

"Does it show?" he asked.

"Every day of your life." She smiled. "Thanks for everything, Stuart. You've been one of the greatest things that ever happened to me!" She stood on her tiptoes and kissed him on the cheek.

"There's the signal," she said. "Are you ready?"

"Sure, but you might have to help me remember what to do."

"You'll remember. It's not like this was your first wedding," she said under her breath as they began to walk up the aisle.

"Well," he said trying to smile at those who turned to gawk at Velvet, "it's the first time I've ever given the bride away!"

"Relax, Brannon, you sound like a nervous father."

"I can tell you one thing," he added, "you make a beautiful bride."

Nodding at the guests, she continued to lead him down the aisle. "Why, Stuart, you're five months late for flattery."

TWO

El Viento pranced as Brannon and Fletcher rode up the trail towards Brighton Pass. The big black horse wanted to race, but most of the road was a series of mud slides and slick rocks.

Brannon himself was in no hurry. The creeks were high. The trees budded out. The clouds scattered and harmless. The sky a pure, clean blue. The sun warming. The wind cooling. The birds singing.

Except for the constant stinging of a knife scratch on his back, a bruised wrist, and a swollen left eye, Brannon considered it a nearly perfect day.

The two men rode their horses at a walk, side by side along the trail. Brannon's Winchester lay across his lap. His coat was completely unbuttoned, and his eyes scanned the trail ahead.

Edwin Fletcher wore a new light jacket, with only the top button fastened. His face was clean shaven, except for a small mustache. His broad-rimmed hat pushed far back on his head, he was reading a newspaper as he rode.

"I say, Brannon . . . listen to this!" Fletcher began. "You haven't read the news, have you?"

"What?" Brannon laughed. "You never let it

out of your sight until the ink's worn off!"

"Well, a man needs to keep current," Fletcher insisted. "Even you might be interested in this:

"Tres Casas celebrated its largest wedding in recent memory last Saturday afternoon when Miss Velvet Wendell, proprietor of the Davis & Wendell Hotel in this city, married Dr. Nelson Shepherd, our beloved doctor and mayor.

"Now comes the good part . . ." Fletcher chuckled.

"The wedding was delayed slightly by Sheriff Brannon who was distracted by some official business only moments before the hour when nuptial commitments were slated to commence. Our sheriff, in one of his last days in office, did appear in time to present the bride. This paper has learned, through reliable sources, that Sheriff Brannon and Miss Wendell's father have been close friends for a number of years. Miss Wendell wore —"

"Her father!" Brannon groaned. "She's a year or two older than I am! Who told them that? Her father's been dead for years!"

Fletcher nodded. "I thought that might amuse you. Actually I liked the part about your being distracted on official business. Shall I read the rest?"

"Not to me . . . knew her father?" Brannon kept mumbling.

"Oh, my word," Fletcher mumbled, "how tragic."

"The wedding?"

"No." Fletcher pointed to the paper he was holding. "There's trouble over in Lincoln County. An English chap by the name of John Turnstall was shot down near his ranch. Did you know a Mr. Turnstall?"

"Afraid not. He's not a relative of yours?" Brannon asked.

"No, poor fellow. It's some kind of a land feud, so they say. Anyway, some of Turnstall's friends have sworn revenge."

"Who are his friends? Maybe I know them," Brannon quizzed.

"It says here, Alexander McSween, John Chisum, and William Bonney."

"I know old John Chisum; he's got a big spread right along the Pecos," Brannon reported. "Never heard of the other two."

"Do you think we should ride down there after we finish our business in the mountains? I mean, the death of an Englishman — it should be investigated," Fletcher suggested.

"That's why they've got a sheriff in Lincoln County. Bradley, or Brady . . . something like that. I met him once down at Santa Fe. He can take care of it without our meddling."

29

"Yes. Quite right," Fletcher mused. "Oh, here's another note:

"Feeling the present name much too negative, the residents of Massacre Meadow voted to change the name of their town. Mayor Dixon Rutherford had campaigned for the name Rutherford City to honor his brothers who were slain in the meadow the previous winter. After a vigorous debate at a town meeting where insults and threats were delivered by all present, the townspeople selected the name Paradise Meadow."

"They have a town and a mayor? A Rutherford is mayor?" Brannon scoffed.

"Are you planning an impeachment campaign?" Fletcher asked.

"Not me, I'm not on the peck. I really don't care what they decide up there. All we need to do is pay our respects to the Mulroneys and leave them Stephen's share of the mine. We'll be pulling out for Arizona by the first of next week. Besides, there can't be more than a couple dozen folks up there anyway."

"I suppose you're right," Fletcher conceded.

Rose Creek blinked her eyes open and stared at the cobwebs in the corner of her canvas ceiling.

They will not defeat me again.

They could not defeat me at Park Hill, Indian Territory.

They could not defeat me in San Bernardino, California.

They cannot defeat me in Paradise Meadow, Colorado.

Her lecture completed, Rose pulled herself out of the small cot that served as her bed, pulled up the wool blankets, and neatly folded back flannel sheets.

Her morning ritual reflected the years of training at the Cherokee National Female Seminary. She had learned arithmetic, philosophy, chemistry, Latin, physical culture, housekeeping, and, of course, Biblical studies. She felt adequately trained to be a schoolteacher.

But "Fem Sem" did not train her how to face an entire community that considered her half-breed Indian heritage a disqualification for teaching their children.

"Most of the parents can't even read and write!" Rose sulked as she stoked her wood stove that served to cook her meals and warm the room.

On the first day of classes last September, Rose had nineteen students in her class. On December first, she had publicly humiliated Mayor Dixon Rutherford by showing up at a town meeting and complaining to the citizenry that she did not appreciate his inappropriate advances. "Mayor Rutherford's moral example is appalling and is a negative influence on the children of this community," she raged.

In response Rutherford, after checking into Creek's Cherokee background, began a drive to have her removed as teacher. In a slightly drunken but impassioned Christmas Eve speech he had declared, "This very meadow, this very town is built on the slaughter of brave men by treacherous savages and half-breeds. We cannot slander the memory of our town's pioneers with such an intolerable situation as this!"

That speech, plus threats of retaliation by those who failed to comply, brought the number of Rose's students down to only three — Sean, Stephen, and Sarah Mulroney. La Plata County officials refused to reassign Miss Creek because they had no one who wanted to serve the rough mining supply camp at Paradise Meadow, and they had no alternate position to offer her.

So for months Rose had taught the three Mulroney children and grimaced as resentment towards her grew. Only the Mulroneys and freight company owner Wishy Boswick would give her more than a two-word conversation. It was Boswick who saw that she kept properly supplied throughout the long, snowbound winter.

Now she was in jeopardy of losing even her three students. Six days previous, Janie Mulroney was run down and killed by a stampeding freight wagon. Accusations flew as to whether the accident could have been avoided. Some said that Mrs. Mulroney had been incensed at Mayor Rutherford and screamed at him up and down Del Oro Street prior to her accident. Others said Mrs. Mulroney, who at times was noted for erratic behavior, ran in front of the runaway wagon on purpose.

Rose had just finished dressing and pulling her long black hair behind her head when she heard shouts from the front of the canvas-topped building that doubled as living quarters and schoolroom.

"Miss Rose! Miss Rose!" a young voice cried. "Come quick, they put Daddy in jail!"

Sticking just her head outside the tent flap door, she glanced down to see six-year-old Sarah Mulroney, still in a nightgown and barefoot, standing in the mud.

"Miss Rose! Some men came this morning and arrested Daddy! They put him in the jail, and they might hang him! You've got to stop them!"

"What?" She opened up the door and scooted Sarah inside. "Who arrested him?"

"You know, Mr. Rutherford . . . and Mr. Hughes, and some of them!"

"Why? What did he do?"

"They said he shot a man!" she whimpered.

"Where are Sean and Stephen?"

"Waiting at the jail. Miss Rose, you've got to help us!"

The Paradise Meadow jail was located in one of the few log buildings in the town. It had been the original stage stop, but when the barn, attached to one end of the cabin, caught fire and partially burned, the stage line had moved to another location. Iron bars were bolted into the interior of the cabin, creating two cells not much larger than a small pantry. In between, about the size of a narrow hall, was the town marshal's office. Most residents did not know the marshal because Rutherford seemed to appoint a different one each week.

With one hand Rose held her long dress high above the mud as she stormed across the rutted meadow that served as a street. In her other hand she carried an unopened parasol resting on her shoulder. An armed gunman stopped her in front of the jail.

"You cain't go in there!" he called.

"I need to talk to Mr. Mulroney!" she demanded.

"Don't get no talkin'," the man replied. "He done shot Loredo! Besides, this ain't no Injun jail."

If the man had been observant, he could have seen the fire building in her eyes.

"Listen, your inane vocabulary and prejudice concern me very little, but I am going to talk to Mr. Mulroney about his children!"

"Nope. Rutherford said absolutely no visitors!"

"Then if you insist, hand me your firearm, and I will guard the prisoner while you take these children home, bathe them, dress them, and cook them some breakfast! Children, go with this man."

"Now, wait jist a minute," he grumbled.

"Well, if you aren't going to do that, I suggest that you take these three Mulroney children to Rutherford and tell him they are his responsibility to raise!" she shouted.

"I cain't . . . I mean —"

"Then," she insisted, "I'm going in!" Miss Rose swished past the guard who reached out to grab her arm but felt the sharp metal point of the unopened parasol stick into his ribs.

"You jist want to talk about them kids?" he gasped.

"That is what I said," she snapped.

"Well . . . that cain't hurt nothin' I suppose." He stepped back and opened the door. "Now listen here, breed, you jist talk to Mulroney . . . you don't go sayin' nothin' to them twins, you understand?"

She barged into the jail.

"Miss Rose!" Peter Mulroney called as she stepped to the iron-barred door. "The children? What have they done with the children?"

"Nothing, apparently. But they're worried sick about you. What happened?"

"Last night, I couldn't take it anymore . . . what with my Janie gone. I went over to Rutherford to confront him about her death. I know he was in on it. Well, he was in that place of his, shouting it out with some other man I've never seen. Anyway, I called him out. Well, one of them fired a shot right through the canvas. I fired back and hit the lantern, which crashed to the floor. Several more shots went off, but I ran back to my place. I figured nothing came of it. Then they showed up this morning and said that I shot some friend of Rutherford's named Loredo and arrested me."

"What are you going to do?"

"I don't know. I know I didn't shoot anybody! But if he dies, they'll go over there and get drunk and come back and hang me!" Mulroney moaned. "They want to kill us all."

"All who?" Creek asked.

"All who know the truth about the hard winter."

"Hard winter? What do you mean?"

"It doesn't matter." He sighed. "The children . . . they matter!"

"What can I do?" she asked.

"Get the children to Brannon!"

"Who?"

"Stuart Brannon. He's got a mine up above us in the mountains northeast of here. If you can find him, he will know what to do."

"Brannon? Is he a relative?" she asked.

"Yes . . . no . . . no, just a partner . . . friend. Just find Brannon!"

"But where is he?"

"I don't know!" Mulroney shook his head. "I should have listened to Janie! We should have gone home to Dublin!"

"Mr. Mulroney, where is this Brannon?" she insisted.

"A gold mine . . . in the mountains!" he muttered.

"Where is the mine? How far away? Is it up on the Little Yellowjacket?"

"I don't know." Mulroney paced the floor. "The photographer! You know . . . Miller? His assistant said they had been to the mine."

"Mr. Mulroney, if you like, I'll take care of the children until we find this Brannon or until you are freed."

"Obliged, Miss Rose." She could see tears rolling down the frightened Irishman's face. "Brannon will know," he repeated, "Brannon will know!"

Miss Creek spun around and trooped out the door. The guard at the door jumped back as she lowered her parasol. Scooping up the children, she marched back to the school. Then, sitting them at their benches, she began to explain.

"Children, your father's doing fine, but we must get him help. He seemed to think Mr. Stuart Brannon could assist in this matter. Do you know a Mr. Brannon?"

"Yes, Miss Rose," Stephen replied.

"Who is this Brannon?"

"He shoots people!" Sean smiled.

"Sean! He does not!" Sarah protested.

"He does too. I saw him!"

Rose looked at Sean. "Is he a gunman then?"

"No!" Sarah answered. "He's a very nice man who took care of us last winter when we were lost in the snow. He told us stories and let us ride his horse —"

"And he shot some bad men right out here in this meadow!" Sean added.

"They was real bad men," Stephen added.

"He was in on that massacre?" Rose gasped.

"Daddy said there wasn't any massacre. Those Rutherfords tried to kill us, and we just

37

shot back. That's what our daddy says," Sarah added.

"So that's what your father meant!" Miss Rose walked silently to the back of the tent, opened a large trunk, and then closed it quickly. "Sean?"

"Yes, ma'am?"

"I need you to try to find Mr. Boswick. He was to go back to Tres Casas, but he might still be in town. Tell him this is an emergency! Stephen, you and Sarah come with me. We need to look for that man who takes the photographs, you know, Hawthorne Miller."

"Miss Rose?" Stephen asked. "I'm awful hungry."

"I'm not dressed proper," Sarah whined.

"Yes, yes . . . of course. Let's eat; then we will look for the others. Sarah, you run home and get dressed. I'll prepare breakfast. Wear some shoes today!"

"Yes, ma'am," Sarah chirped as she darted from the tent.

"Is that man . . . you know, the one that got shot, going to die?" Stephen asked.

"We should pray for him," Sean offered.

"Well," Miss Rose stammered, "I'm a little busy right now. So why don't you two pray for him?"

Pray? she pondered. *Just like I prayed my father wouldn't die of smallpox? Just like I prayed that they wouldn't kill all our cows? Just like I prayed for a chance to study at Mount Holyoke? Just like I prayed for Jimmy?*

Paradise Meadow looked more like a shipwreck than a town. White tent buildings rose out of the stacks and stacks of crates and cartons that had made it through Brighton Pass but had not yet been shipped up to the mines. There were few organized streets, and where the ground was visible, it consisted of gummy clay mud. Teams of mules, horses, and oxen struggled to haul freight from place to place.

Along the edges of the meadow, crews worked felling trees and putting up cabins, stores, and saloons. Most of the best buildings had split-log floors, wooden walls, and canvas roofs.

Crusty old miners were starting to filter in from their claims. Storekeepers, barbers, lawyers, gamblers, and soiled doves had streamed up from Tres Casas to open up business.

To find someone you almost had to search the whole town, because chances were they would not be located in the same place as on the previous day.

After scraping their breakfast plates clean, Miss Rose and two of the Mulroney children started out for the far side of town where several buildings were taking shape.

With several inches of mud stuck to her high-top, lace-up black shoes, she made it to the construction but could not find Hawthorne Miller. One member of the crew thought she would find Miller over by the creek. There were rumors of a party of Utes camped nearby, and they thought Miller had headed in that direction.

Reaching the stream, they crossed a log foot-bridge and passed through a grove of aspen towards Mr. Miller's wagon. There was no one in sight. Miss Rose called out to him.

A grumbling noise slipped out from under the black shanty with canvas doors perched atop the wagon.

"Mr. Miller, may I have a word with you?" she called out.

"Busy . . . too busy . . . come back later!" came the muffled reply.

"Mr. Miller, I really must speak with you!" she called.

Suddenly a head poked out of the canvas flaps. Covering his eyes with his hand, Miller squinted in the sunlight.

"Miss Rose! Did you change your mind about wearing buckskins and posing with the children?" he bellowed.

"I certainly did not!"

"Very well," he muttered and disappeared back into the portable dark room.

"Mr. Miller, I need some information, please! Do you know a Mr. Stuart Brannon?" she shouted.

Suddenly Hawthorne Miller stuck his head back out of the tent. "Did you say Brannon?"

"Yes," she called, "I must get a message to Mr. Brannon."

Miller stepped out of the tent and awkwardly climbed off the wagon.

"Say," he mumbled, "wouldn't that be a picture? Legendary gunman Stuart Brannon with a half-breed in buckskins, my yes. Carry on, Gilmore!" he shouted back.

"All I need to know," she said, "is the location of Mr. Brannon's mine. The children's father has been arrested, and this doesn't help. You know Brannon, I presume?"

"Know him? The uncultured ruffian! Ruthless, that's what he is. Yes, we've had a confrontation. Of course, I lived through it; that's more than many a man can say!"

"What kind of man is he?"

"A violent, unpredictable man, that's what. One minute he asks you to dine, and the next he attempts to pistol-whip you. Take my advice, Miss Rose, do not get mixed up with this fellow."

"Do you know where his claim is?" she demanded.

"Of course I do. One of the few in this town to ever be at the Brannon claim. The Little Stephen Mine, I believe he calls it."

"That's me!" Stephen shouted. "That's my mine! I mean, I'm one of the partners!"

"You don't say . . . Little Stephen of the Little Stephen. Now wouldn't that have been grand, if he would have let me photograph the mine."

"Please, just tell us where the mine is!" she pressed.

"Well, I suppose I could be persuaded to tell what I know," he pondered.

"What do you mean, persuaded?"

"Well, you agree to pose in buckskins next to Brannon, and I'll give you directions to the mine."

Creek's gaze froze, and she could feel the temples of her forehead tightening. She had been in this same squeeze before. Far too many times to let it pass!

She shoved the pointed end of her parasol at Miller, then addressed Stephen and Sarah who were standing at her side.

"Children, take a good look at Mr. Miller. It's not every day that you see such a sorry excuse for a man. Perhaps the Almighty made a few errors in constructing him; you'll notice that his speech is incoherent and his brain seems to be made of buffalo dung!"

The children giggled.

"Well! I can see you half-breeds are no better than Brannon himself!" he huffed. Immediately he climbed back upon the wagon and went into the dark room.

Miss Rose turned and sighed.

Nice going, Creek. You showed him. Of course it won't help the children in the least!

"Maybe Sean has found Mr. Boswick," Sarah offered.

She nodded her head and led them back to the footbridge.

"Miss Rose! Ma'am! Wait up!"

She turned to see a young man running after them from Miller's wagon. Catching his breath,

42

he glanced to see if anyone was watching.

"I'm Jeremiah Gilmore, Mr. Miller's assistant. I heard your conversation."

"Can you tell us where the mine is? Where is this Brannon?"

"I can tell you where the mine was. But that won't do you any good." He shrugged. "The Ute hunters that came to town this week were trading mining gear. They said 'the Brannon' gave the mine to them when he left the mountains last fall."

"Did they say where he went?"

"No."

"Look, Mr. Gilmore, we —"

"Jeremy, ma'am. Just call me Jeremy." He pulled his hat off his head, brushed back his hair and smiled.

"Jeremy," she said, "it is extremely important to find Brannon. If you hear anything about him, could you let me know?"

"Yes, ma'am! You can count on me." He blushed.

"How old are you, Jeremy?" she asked.

"Almost eighteen, ma'am!"

Eighteen? Maybe sixteen! That a girl, Creek. You're a real charmer if they're only children.

"Eh, Jeremy, tell me about Brannon. Some people think he's a murderer, and others think he's a hero. What do you say?"

"Ma'am, all I know is that he's a very tough hombre. He won't back down from no one, no ma'am. He told me the real story of the shootout

43

at Paradise Meadow, and it sure ain't what you hear around here."

"Would he stand up against Rutherford and his kind?"

"Yes, ma'am, I believe he would."

"Well, thank you for your help. Let's hope we find him in time." She smiled and offered her hand.

He wiped his hand on his shirt, then rapidly shook hers.

As they crossed the footbridge to return to town, it was Sarah who spoke first.

"I think Jeremiah Gilmore likes you, Miss Rose!"

"Yes, that's nice. There don't seem to be many in town that feel the same."

"No," Sarah said giggling, "I mean he really, really likes you!"

"That's dumb," Stephen broke in. "He's young and Miss Rose is an old lady!"

Creek wasn't going to smile, but she couldn't help but laugh at Stephen's innocent gaze.

"You're right about that, young man. Now let's find Sean and see what he knows."

On their third day out Brannon and Fletcher crested Brighton Pass about noon and slowly worked their way past others on the trail. The road to Paradise Meadow was crowded with freight wagons struggling through the muddy snow-melt-filled ruts. Brannon and Fletcher

44

branched off towards the creek to find a place to bed down for the night. Then a sudden downpour sent them scurrying for the cover of the trees and their yellow slickers.

"I say, Stuart, wouldn't this be the place we found Mrs. Mulroney and the others?"

"Could be. It looks a lot different without the snow."

Within moments the thunderous downpour subsided, and the evening sun broke through the rolling clouds. Brannon began to gather a few sticks and scratch out a fire circle.

"Edwin, let's pitch camp here. Listen, are you sufficiently through with that newspaper?"

"My heavens, are you actually going to read it?"

"Why should I? You've read every word to me at least three times!" Brannon laughed. "I just figured it would make starting a wet fire a little easier."

"Well," Fletcher mumbled, "I suppose that would be a good use. Of course, I did tear out the mention of the wedding. And the part about Turnstall. Oh, yeah, and the bit about the Bland-Allison Act being passed over the veto of President Hayes."

"Is there any newspaper left?"

"Oh, yes . . . quite!" Fletcher handed Brannon the tatters.

"Well," Brannon said laughing, "at least the obituaries are intact. I don't remember you reading those."

"I never read obituaries," he admitted.

45

"You never read obituaries?" Brannon questioned.

"Never."

"Why?"

"Eh . . . call it superstition, I suppose. I just choose not to read obituaries," he replied. "Old family tradition. Fletchers never read obituaries."

Brannon squatted to build the fire and began to wad up the paper.

"Well, I suppose you didn't miss —" Suddenly, Brannon stood straight up.

"Edwin!" he shouted. "Listen!

"Reports have reached Tres Casas concerning the accidental death of Jane Mulroney, residing in Paradise Meadow (formally Massacre Meadow), La Plata County, Colorado. She was one of the few citizens to dwell in the region before last summer's mining boom. According to Dr. C. Stover, Mrs. Mulroney suffered severe internal injury when run down by a runaway freight wagon and team. She is survived by her husband, Peter, and several children."

"My word, Brannon, is that? . . . of course . . . how horrid!"

"Janie! It has to be Janie Mulroney." Brannon gazed off into the distance.

An easily terrified woman meeting a terrifying death. Lord, that just doesn't seem right!

"I say, how will Peter handle those children?"

Fletcher mumbled.

"I suppose we will find that out tomorrow." Brannon squatted back down and continued to build a fire. But his mind traveled back to deep snows of a winter past and a cabin crowded with people.

THREE

Twelve months can change a man.

He can go from a child to a man. From poor to rich. From young to old. From laughing to crying. From strong to weak.

And twelve months can change a region, too.

Especially if gold and silver have been discovered nearby.

There was little to remind Brannon and Fletcher that the clearing they approached was once just a deep snowfield in front of the stage stop at Broken Arrow Crossing.

Surveying the mad confusion from a distance, Fletcher stood in his stirrups.

"It looks like the first wave of civilization has washed ashore at Paradise Meadow," he announced.

"Humanity is here," Brannon mused. "Whether it is civil or not remains to be seen."

"Is that the cabin over on the far side?"

Brannon, too, stood in his stirrups. "Where's the barn? Did they tear it down?"

"That road is so packed with wagons, I don't know if we can find a lane to ride down," Fletcher observed.

Brannon smiled. "Come on, Edwin, let's rim the edge of the trees and circle town. Maybe we will spot Mulroney."

"Might I suggest we just post him the funds and bypass this turmoil completely?"

"Sure," Brannon said laughing, "just where do you suppose the post office is?"

Two men leading pack mules approached. Brannon called to them, "Would you mind pointing us towards the post office?"

"Cain't hep ya," one called back. "Just pulled into town ourselves. Say, you don't happen to know where a man kin git a shave and a bath, do ya?"

"Sorry." Brannon shrugged.

Glancing back he noticed a man who had been asleep on some tarp-covered crates sit up and squint his eyes at them.

"Say," Brannon said pulling off his hat and wiping his brow, "where's the post office around here?"

The man cleared his throat and pulled some makings out of his vest pocket. "Well, it used to be down next to the Bull's Tail Saloon, but they moved it this week, and I ain't figured out where they put it!"

"Do you know Peter Mulroney?" Brannon asked.

"Nope." The man stuck the quirley between his lips and searched for a match. "Do you know Sammy Soogan?" he countered.

"Afraid not," Brannon replied.

Then the man lay back down on the goods. "Well, if you see him, tell him I'm still over here with the outfit."

Brannon just nodded his head and rode on.

Working their way between freight wagons and prospectors, mules and packing crates, they wound around the outskirts of town. Every trail, path, and crooked street was knotted with excited crowds of men, animals, and goods.

"I say." Fletcher motioned. "Over there . . . what's the pandemonium?"

Brannon looked up to see a large crowd moving towards the trees on the west side of town. They spurred their horses and tried to see the source of commotion. So many people kept barging in front of them that progress was slow.

"What's happening up ahead?" Fletcher called out to one man.

"A hanging!" came the shouted reply.

"And you didn't think law and order had come to Paradise Meadow," Fletcher commented.

"He didn't say anything about law and order. Just a hanging."

"Are we going?" Fletcher turned in the saddle to address Brannon.

"I've seen them before. How about you, Edwin? Have you ever seen a hanging?"

"I should say not. And I don't intend on witnessing this one unless you insist."

"Not me. This time we'll let their law handle their own problems."

"I say, that doesn't sound like Sheriff Brannon!"

"Cattleman Brannon. I'm on my way back to

my Arizona ranch, remember?" Brannon reminded.

"Are you sure you're not just in a hurry to get to visit a certain lady in Prescott?" Fletcher kidded.

Brannon turned and scowled. "The middle of town seems to have thinned out; let's cut across to the cabin. I presume Mulroney is still living at Broken Arrow Station."

Passing by a completed building and several large tent-walled structures, Brannon was startled to hear someone yelling at him.

"Hey! You — on the black horse — hey! Stop!"

Instinctively as he turned in the saddle, his right hand went to the polished wooden handle of his revolver.

A dark-skinned woman clothed in a long print dress waved an unopened parasol at him. Her hair was tied behind her head, but she didn't wear a hat.

"You! On the black horse! Are you the worthless marshal we're stuck with this week?"

Brannon looked around at the tents and crates. "Me?"

"Yeah . . . you! The brave man who has to have his hand on a revolver when he talks to women. They told me that Rutherford's new marshal rode a black horse."

"Well, ma'am, we just arrived in town, and I'm not the marshal." He tipped his hat.

"Not yet, anyway," Fletcher kidded.

51

"Then you do work for Rutherford?" she probed.

"Not likely."

"Are you a prospector?" she asked.

"Retired prospector," Brannon admitted.

"You going into business in Paradise Meadow?"

"Nope."

"Great, more two-bit gamblers and gunmen," she moaned. "That's just what we need."

He motioned towards the crowd. "Who's getting hung?"

"No one, if I can help it!" she barked. "Do you two know how to use those guns, or do they just hold up your britches?"

"I say, Stuart, is this woman mad?"

"Look, Mr. Stuart, or whatever your name is, in about ten minutes those illegitimate jackals are going to hang an innocent man who wasn't even allowed to explain his case! So either come along and plan on using those pistols, or lend them to me so I can try to keep the children of this God-forsaken community from having to witness a hanging!"

"And who are you?" Brannon quizzed.

"Give me your hand and pull me up. Take me over to that crowd."

"My word, is she serious?" Fletcher asked.

"Are you Ute?" Brannon asked.

"I happen to be Miss Rose Creek, the school-teacher in Paradise Meadow. My parental background is absolutely no concern of yours. Nor is yours any concern of mine. But I am not ashamed to be Cherokee."

Brannon pulled her up behind him on El Viento. "Cherokee? Why out in Colorado?"

"May I remind you, Mr. Stuart," she lectured, "there are no racial travel restrictions here."

"Look, relax, lady. I'll take you to the crowd. Now what's the name of this man that's about to be hung?"

"I don't know."

"You don't know? You expect us to march into a wild —"

"I don't know his name. He's Indian. Ute, I presume. All I know is they dragged him across town and hollered that they were hanging an Indian thief."

"Why doesn't the marshal stop them?"

"Because the marshal, whoever he is this week, works for Rutherford."

"Rutherford wants this Indian hung?"

"Obviously."

"Well, Miss Creek, you can count us in, right, Fletcher?"

"Actually, I don't suppose I have a choice in the matter," he mumbled. *"Alea iacta est!"*

"I would hardly call this the Rubicon," Creek retorted; then she slapped El Viento's rump with her parasol. The fiery black started to bolt, and only Brannon's hard jerk on the rein refrained him. Instead, the horse whinnied and reared, causing Miss Creek to clutch Brannon in desperation. However, the crowd on the street in front of them scurried to safety leav-

53

ing them a path forward.

Brannon kept the horse moving, and the crowd begrudgingly parted before them. He could see that a huge log had been hoisted up and jammed in the forks of two trees, providing a sturdy cross timber from which hung a noose.

He turned to say something to the schoolteacher, but she had slipped off the horse and was shoving her way into the clearing. Brannon and Fletcher watched as she ran out to the men who led a bruised Indian on the end of a rope.

"Wait!" Brannon heard her yell. "Give him a chance to explain himself!"

"Looks like the Indians and breeds stick together!" one of the men on horseback shouted. "I told you we'd have trouble with a schoolteacher like this! If we show this one a lesson, the others will learn!"

"Rutherford?" Fletcher asked.

"That would be my guess." Brannon gently pulled his Winchester from its scabbard and shoved in a couple more shells. Then he pulled his coat away from his handgun.

"You going to use those?" Fletcher called above the noise of the crowd.

"Maybe." With his right index finger on the trigger, he laid the rifle across his lap.

"You've got to listen to his explanation!" Miss Creek shouted.

"He cain't speak English!" one man shouted.

"That's the point! We must wait for an interpreter!" she screamed. "He deserves a fair trial!"

"Breeds and Indians don't deserve nothin'," Rutherford shouted waving his hat at the crowd. "He was riding a stolen horse and trying to sell stolen mining equipment. All of you who think he ought to hang, say 'aye.'"

A loud roar rolled out of the crowd.

"All those who think this buck ought to wait and stand trial, holler 'no.'"

Miss Creek began to yell, "Wait!" but the blast of Brannon's rifle interrupted her scream. The bullet sizzled through Rutherford's raised hat, causing it to fly through the air. Several men drew guns on Brannon, but his raised Winchester and the crowd of people around where he sat kept them from shooting.

"Let the Indian speak!" Brannon shouted. Never lowering his sights from Rutherford, he rode into the clearing with Fletcher, gun drawn, following behind.

"I say, Brannon," Fletcher whispered under his breath, "isn't that poor chap one of Red Shirt's friends?"

"Just who do you think you are, Mister?" Rutherford shouted furiously.

"I'm the man who traded that horse to Chalco!"

"Who's Chalco?"

"The man you're about to hang!" Brannon announced.

"That weren't your horse," one of Rutherford's men hollered.

Miss Creek walked over and began untying the Indian as Brannon continued.

"The man who rode that horse was killed in a gunfight. I fed the horse, and no one came to claim it, so I traded it to this Ute."

"How do we know you're telling the truth, Mister?" someone shouted.

"You don't. But if you'll pull back the long hair on that left front pastern, you'll find the scar of a two-inch cut!" Brannon barked.

"I hope you know what you're doing," Fletcher muttered under his breath.

One of Rutherford's men dismounted and looked at the Indian's horse.

"He's right!" he called.

"If this horse belongs to any man here, just come up and pay me the livery charge, and I'll give you the money for the horse!"

No one claimed the horse, and many in the crowd, sensing a possible gunfight, began to slip back into Paradise Meadow. Rutherford dismounted, retrieved his hat, and tried to stand where Brannon's rifle was not pointed directly at him. "What about that prospecting gear; he obviously stole that!" he shouted. "This savage probably killed some poor prospector!"

"I gave it all to Chief Ouray himself. I suggest you give this man his trade goods so the Chief doesn't need to bring the whole tribe down here and collect!"

"He's not getting one thing in Paradise Meadow," Rutherford stated.

"Then let him ride out of here with his goods," Brannon insisted.

Brannon could see a man standing next to Rutherford shift from one foot to the other. He rubbed his palms together and brushed them on his vest.

He's going to draw . . . not in this crowd!

"Folks," Brannon called out, "especially you standing behind that man with the dirty brown hat next to Rutherford. I'm going to ask you to move. That old boy is just about to draw his gun and take a shot at me. Well, the slug from this Winchester will go clean through his body and hit some of you. Or maybe it will hit a bone and ricochet out of him in who knows what direction. So unless you all want in this fight, I'd suggest you just move way back out of the way."

"He's bluffin'!" the man cried out.

"Ain't no man going to ride in here and bully us!" another called.

"Of course not," Creek added, "that's what we have a mayor for."

"Come on, folks, get out of here!" Brannon called.

People started scattering.

"You ain't riding out of town!" the nervous man called.

By now there were no more than a dozen men scattered around Rutherford. Chalco mounted his horse. He rode over by Brannon and Fletcher.

"Miss Creek, you clear out of here now," Brannon ordered.

"So you men can slaughter each other?" she

protested. "This is Paradise Meadow, not Abilene!"

"Ma'am, they are going to shoot. I can't stop them from doing that. But maybe I can keep you from taking a bullet."

"Oh, this is great," she yelled, "this is just great! I get rescued from some gun-crazy idiots by another gun-crazy idiot. Is there any possibility that any of you have the brain power to solve your differences without shooting someone?" Turning towards Rutherford, she said, "Mayor, go back to your place and let these men ride away."

"Mister," Rutherford shouted as he turned to leave, "if you ever show up at Paradise Meadow again, I'll have you arrested."

Suddenly, the whole gang mounted up and rode back into town leaving Brannon, Fletcher, Creek, and Chalco next to the log with the noose.

"Look," she informed Brannon, "Stuart, or whoever you are, I appreciate your stepping in to stop this lynching, but with your temper and your trigger finger, I think it would best for you to just ride off. We don't need more gunfights in Paradise Meadow."

"Do you know how to speak Ute?" he asked her.

"No, do you?" she hammered right back. "I can speak Cherokee, Latin, and some French, but not Ute. Look, get him out of here. Those men will drink some courage and come back wanting to shoot."

"Fletcher, give Chalco our grub bag and that new jacket of yours; I'll give him a few bullets and a folding knife."

"I say, what? My jacket?"

"He can't go back to Ouray empty-handed! Besides the jacket makes you look squirrely."

"Squirrely? You don't say? But —"

"Chalco, my friend," Brannon said to the Indian, "Red Shirt is my friend. These are for you!" He handed the supplies to the Indian who managed a frightened smile.

Before he could say another word, a shot rang out from the trees, and Chalco tumbled off his horse with a scream. Brannon, still holding the Winchester, dove to the ground pulling Rose Creek down with him. She came up with a right cross to Brannon's chin that sent him rolling backwards.

"Don't you ever —" she began.

Brannon didn't have time to even listen to her indignation. Another shot whizzed above their heads.

"Edwin, get the horses out of here! Miss Creek, check on Chalco; I think he took lead . . . stay down!"

A third bullet hit about four feet in front of Brannon and buried itself in the mud. But this time he was ready. Spotting the gunman back in the trees, he fired three quick shots and then dove behind one of the trees supporting the hanging log.

Another bullet shattered branches and bark

above his head. Brannon sat behind the tree and waited for another shot. After a moment, a bullet drilled its way into the tree trunk, and Brannon rolled from behind the tree firing two quick shots at the sniper. The man dropped to the pine needles and mud with a scream.

Brannon waited to see if there was another gunman. Sensing a crowd starting to gather near the clearing, he cautiously moved straight at the fallen gunman. The man clutched his right shoulder.

"Don't shoot me again!" the man pleaded.

"Do you want me to be merciful like you were to the Indian?" Brannon yelled. "Who are you?"

"Nobody . . . get me a doctor!"

Brannon watched the man glance over to where he had dropped his rifle. "Who're you working for?"

"Nobody . . . I've got to stop this bleeding."

Brannon laid the barrel of the Winchester against the man's good shoulder. "I want to know why you were doing this!" he shouted.

"Dixon!" the man stammered. "Dixon said he'd give one hundred dollars to any man who would shoot you or the Indian."

"Who was with you?"

"Nobody."

Brannon shoved the rifle barrel a little deeper into the man's shoulder.

"Cleve . . . Cleve, the one in the brown hat!" he shouted. "Get me a doc!"

Kneeling down, Brannon scooped up the man's hat, rolled it, and propped it under his head for a pillow. Then pulling off the wounded man's blue bandana, he folded it and pressed it into the wound.

"Listen . . . hold that tight and stop the bleeding; I'll go get you some help."

The wounded man just nodded.

Brannon turned back to the clearing and had only taken three steps when he heard a hammer click. Rolling in the mud to his right just as a shot rang out, he fired two quick rounds at the wounded gunman who was now propped on his elbow and still held a smoking pistol in his hand.

This time when he collapsed, he didn't move.

Why? Brannon stood to his feet. *It doesn't make sense. For a hundred dollars? The world's going crazy, Lord, this whole world is crazy.*

Fletcher ran to Brannon's side, with pistol drawn.

"Stuart! Are you wounded?"

"He didn't need to die." Brannon shook his head. "Why do they do that, Fletcher?"

"Chalco was hit in the leg, and a crowd is gathering back. We better get out of here quickly," Fletcher advised.

"Get the horses; we're leaving now!" Brannon shouted commands as he ran.

Back at the clearing, Creek had tied a tight bandage around the Indian's wounded leg.

"How is he?" Brannon called.

"Alive . . . now would you three get out of here!" she called.

He shoved the Indian up into the saddle and

slapped the horse's rump. "Take him west, Fletcher; I'll catch up! Where did you get that wrapping?" He nodded at Chalco's bandage.

"It's none of your business," she snapped as she held the bit on El Viento while Brannon mounted. "Did you leave dead bodies lying around out in the woods?"

"Only one."

"How considerate of you."

He dug back through his saddle bags and grabbed the leather pouch. "Schoolteacher, I've got to trust you. Do you know Peter Mulroney?"

"Certainly, he's in —"

"Then give him this money and tell him it's Stephen's share. He'll understand. Tell him what happened and why we can't stay and visit."

"Whom do I tell him this money came from?" she called out.

"Tell him Brannon sent it." He turned El Viento's head and spurred the big black horse. They shot off west with a thunderous gallop.

"Brannon?" she screamed. "You're Brannon?"

But he had disappeared into the woods before she stopped screaming his name. Whipping around towards town, she realized that at least a dozen men had listened to her shouts.

Rose Creek pushed her way through the milling men and hiked across town to the schoolroom. The whole morning had been like a bad dream.

A very bad dream. All I wanted to do was find Mr. Boswick. Why did they have to try to hang that poor fellow? Why did people have to get shot?

Why did that man have to be this Brannon?

She wanted to be alone.

She wanted to lie on her cot and cry.

She wanted to be looking on the green rolling hills of the Indian Nation.

She wanted to be in a safe room at the seminary.

"Miss Rose," Sarah called. "What was the shooting? Did someone get killed? They didn't shoot Daddy, did they?" she cried.

All three children came and hugged her skirt.

"Listen, your father is all right. They were trying to hang an innocent Ute man, and your friend Mr. Brannon stopped them."

"Mr. Brannon's here?" Stephen shouted.

"He was here, but he rode off —" she began.

"Isn't he going to help us?" Sean asked.

"He doesn't know that we need his help. You see, I didn't know it was Mr. Brannon, and I didn't have a chance to tell him about your father."

"He'll come back," Sarah said. "He's our friend."

"Well, he's a very violent man. Perhaps there is another way."

"Did he shoot someone?" Stephen's blue eyes grew large.

"Yes, I believe he did," Miss Rose replied.

"Dead?" Sarah gulped.

"Yes."

"I told ya," Sean announced, "he shoots 'em!"

"Oh." She pulled out the packet of papers Brannon had handed her and began to read them.

"Mr. Brannon gave me this. Children . . . listen. Stephen's share of the gold mine is $2,500!"

"Is that the money?" Sarah asked.

"No, no, it just says that the money is in a bank in Tres Casas and can be collected whenever you go to town."

"Is that a lot of money, Miss Rose?" Stephen asked.

"Yes, indeed it is."

"Maybe if we give it to Rutherford, he'll let my daddy go," Stephen suggested.

"I doubt it, children." Walking to the back of the room, she picked up her hand mirror. She glanced at her reflection but saw nothing. "I need to go and talk with your father! You stay here and work on —"

"Miss Rose? Miss Rose?"

"Eh, what is it, Stephen?"

"Your face is dirty, ma'am," he offered.

She picked the mirror back up and noticed mud smeared across the cheek and her hair wild and tangled to one side. Looking at her dress, she saw that it too was muddy, and a smear of Chalco's blood streaked the side.

The pride of the Cherokee Nation? If I had a good horse . . . I could steal one. That would impress them. All I ever wanted to do is teach school!

"Children, go fetch some water. I'll change clothes. Hurry now!"

There had been no time to wash yesterday's dress.

Today's was ruined.

She pulled out the dark blue one she had been saving for some special event.

"Nothing special will ever happen in this town. But it's either this or the buckskins," she muttered.

In a few minutes she was mostly clean and clothed.

"You look beautiful, Miss Rose!"

"Thank you, Sarah."

"Someday I'm going to look just like Miss Rose!" Sarah beamed.

"You won't ever look like Miss Rose!" Sean taunted.

"I will too!"

"Will not! You can't!"

"Why can't I?"

" 'Cause you aren't Indian!" Sean blurted out, then quickly covered his mouth with his hand.

All three children stared up at Miss Rose. She realized that it was the first time they had ever made that distinction to her face.

"Well," she smiled, "there are some very beautiful Irish women, you know."

"Like Mamma," Sarah said nodding at the boys.

"Can we come with you, Miss Rose?" Sean asked.

"I think you had better wait here. I don't think it's too safe out there. If Mr. Boswick comes by, tell him where I am," she instructed.

A warm west wind had been blowing all morning, and the mud of the streets of Paradise Meadow had begun to dry. Only the deep ruts held water now. Creek felt overdressed and self-conscious as she walked to the jail.

Several of Rutherford's men sat on the porch in front of the jail.

"Ohheee, Cleve, did you ever think about takin' a squaw for a wife?" She heard one of the men's hoarse laughter. She didn't turn her head, but walked straight to the door.

A man with rifle in hand appeared to block her entrance. "No visitors," he announced.

"Listen," she began, "I must talk to Mr. Mulroney about his children!" She turned to look at the men who now formed a circle about her, searching for the one who had earlier allowed her to go into the jail.

"Where's the man who was on duty this morning?" she demanded.

"Dead."

"What?"

"Yeah, that squaw-man Brannon shot him down. You were there!"

"Maybe she put a slug in old Hughes, too."

"She helped that Indian."

Someone pushed her from behind and she stumbled towards another man.

"He was probably her lover!"

She was tripped and fell to the ground catching her dress on the man's spurs. She heard the blue velvet rip as she slammed against the dirt street. She rolled over to her hands and knees and reached down to draw her knife out of her moccasins.

There was no knife.

There were no moccasins.

It had been years since she had worn either. *Not here! Not now! Not this way!*

A deep booming blast stunned her eardrums and froze every man in his place.

"The next shot will separate your heads from your bodies!" a voice growled.

She looked up to see Wishy Boswick standing behind the men with a double-barreled shotgun in his hand. One man moved his hand towards his pistol.

"Try it, Mister, and they'll be mailing your brains back home from Utah!" Wishy warned. "Miss Rose, are you all right?"

She stood up and tried to brush off her dress. "I've been better, Mr. Boswick."

"Look, Boswick," one of the men stammered, "we was just sportin' with her."

"Miss Rose," Boswick called, "I suggest you leave with me; this is not the safest part of town."

"I believe you're right." She brushed her hair back.

They backed to the corner of the street and cautiously wound their way toward the school.

Still looking back over his shoulder, Boswick spoke. "Miss Rose, it might be prudential for you to leave with me. I can give you a lift to Tres Casas."

"Brannon was here today," she said.

"Brannon? Where is he?"

"Gone west before I could talk to him!"

"West? That's canyon country."

"Mr. Boswick, do you have any way of getting a message to him?"

"Well, I was headed south, but I suppose I could take the long way around. Say, aren't you coming with me?"

"I won't leave the children."

"Things could get nasty here after dark," Boswick cautioned.

"Next time I will be better prepared."

"It don't seem right. You got some friends here in town to stay with?"

"With you gone, the only friend I have is in jail."

"You better come with me."

"Can you get a message to Brannon?"

"I'll try my best."

She walked into the schoolroom and searched for a pencil and paper.

"Miss Rose! What happened to you?" Sarah cried out.

"It's just a bad day for clothes." She tried to smile at the children. Returning to Boswick, she wrote a message and handed it to him.

"This Brannon, he can read, can't he?" she asked.

Boswick nodded. "Yes. Brannon's a good man."

"That remains to be seen," she added. "Mr. Boswick, I have one more extremely big favor to ask. Is it possible for you to leave me the Greener shotgun and some cartridges?"

"Miss Rose?"

"The next time a man shoves me to the ground, he will have eternal regrets!"

"Miss Rose, bring the children with you. Leave Paradise Meadow with me," he offered again.

"My people have been counting on others protecting us for over one hundred years. So far, it's all been a disaster. I'll make my stand right here."

FOUR

Crossing a tree-covered ridge, Brannon, Fletcher, and Chalco began a slow, gradual descent towards the canyon country. They rode single file with the Ute leading and Brannon trailing, always glancing back to see if they were being followed.

After about an hour of steady riding, Brannon signaled for the others to stop. Blood from his gunshot wound was starting to show through Chalco's bandages, but the Indian himself looked strong. He stayed mounted while Fletcher and Brannon got down to drink from a small creek.

The water rushed clear and cold. The milky snow-melt was long gone, and the stagnant pools of summer still weeks away. The grasses greened at the edge of the creek. Future wildflowers stood half grown.

Looking up at the Indian, Brannon motioned with his hands. "Chalco, where's Red Shirt? Red Shirt? . . . *donde esta?*" he pressed.

The Indian looked at Brannon for a long minute. Then he held up two fingers and pointed west.

"Two? Two what?" Fletcher asked.

"Two miles? Two days? Two canyons? Two hours? Two men?" Brannon grilled.

Chalco nodded.

"My word, Stuart, just where are we going?"

Brannon shrugged. "I guess we're going 'two.' "

"You know, I still can't believe you left that money with the schoolteacher." Fletcher adjusted the cinch on his saddle and rubbed the flanks of his sorrel gelding.

Brannon tossed his wide-brimmed black hat over the saddle horn, bent down, splashed the cold water across his square-jawed face, and then ran his fingers through his brown hair. "Yeah, I was thinking the same thing. I mean, it just seemed like the right thing to do at the time."

"She certainly didn't act like a schoolteacher," Fletcher added. "How do we know that she wasn't a —"

"We don't," Brannon interrupted. "All I know is that I saw her stand up single-handed to Dixon Rutherford. That seemed like credentials enough. Still . . . Well, we should have stayed to give our condolences to Mulroney."

"So we're going back?" Fletcher asked.

"I've been thinking about it. I've never been too good at runnin' from conflict. Course we need to see that Chalco makes it to his people."

"I thought that exit was much too simple," Fletcher commented.

"Simple? A near hanging, gunfight, men shot, some dead, running barely ahead of a vigilante mob . . . you call that simple?"

"For the legendary Stuart Brannon," Fletcher exclaimed, "it's just an ordinary day!"

"We'll go back in at night, check with Mulroney, and then slip out before daylight. No need to stir up things," Brannon suggested.

Edwin Fletcher gave Brannon a look of disbelief and then remounted his horse. "Stuart, the day life with you gets dull, I'm sailing back to England."

A few more miles down the western slope of the mountains, just where the firs and spruces began to thin out into scrub cedars and piñon pines, Chalco pulled up on the reins and slipped down off his horse.

"Chalco?" Brannon called.

"I say, what's he doing?"

"Limping, mainly . . . maybe his leg hurts."

Fletcher reached for his canteen. "I believe he's gathering wood for a fire."

Brannon dismounted and tied El Viento to a dead log.

"Well, it's dinner time, and he's got all the food."

"Yes, that was a rather hasty trade. We will need supplies before we go to Arizona," Fletcher cautioned.

"Another reason to go back to town," Brannon nodded.

"Don't remind me."

Using Chalco's newly gained food supply and Brannon's utensils, they soon had coffee boiling and salted meat warming over the coals. They couldn't find any words that Chalco understood besides *eat, Red Shirt,* and *dogs.*

"I can see how Mrs. Mulroney could have gotten run down in Paradise Meadow," Fletcher began. "The derangement in the streets is deplorable!"

"Well, it should settle down soon. With this warm wind blowing, the passes to the mines will open enough to get all that gear hauled on up the hill soon."

"Did you ever think that we could be in that same position?" Fletcher challenged. "If we still had the mine, we'd be trying to move equipment up to the Little Stephen."

"Makes you glad to be leaving the mountains." Brannon nodded.

Fletcher nudged Brannon and pointed toward Chalco on the other side of the fire pit. The Indian stood and began to unwrap his bandage which, even in its soiled state, looked to Brannon like a torn petticoat. Then he rolled up his buckskins above the wounds. Brannon could see that the injury in the front of his leg was fairly small, and the bleeding seemed to have stopped. But the back of the leg, where the bullet exited, revealed a ragged slash still oozing fresh blood.

"My word, that's a nasty injury," Fletcher whispered.

Chalco took his tin coffee cup and refilled it from the pot on the coals.

"Do you think we should do something?" Fletcher began, but Brannon held up his hand to silence him.

The Indian took the hot coffee and splashed

the entire cup on the fresh wound — yowling, hopping around the fire, and gritting his teeth as he did. Then he scooped up the bandage and blotted the wound clean.

"He scalded himself!" Fletcher groaned.

"Well . . . that should cleanse it," Brannon replied.

Chalco then grabbed a stick about two feet long and as thick as his thumb and began to roll a fist-sized rock around in the middle of the coals.

"What's he doing, baking a rock?" Fletcher asked.

"I'd say . . ." Brannon paused and took a deep breath. ". . . that he's going to cauterize that wound."

"My word, with a rock?" Fletcher asked.

"So it seems."

"We can't let him —" Fletcher began.

"It's his leg." Brannon pulled Fletcher back. "The Utes have survived out here a lot longer than we have."

Chalco rolled the hot rock out of the fire pit and put the stick between his teeth, biting down hard. Then he carefully sat down holding his leg wound straight above the nearly glowing rock.

"Good grief, Brannon, he's not —"

Brannon ignored Fletcher but looked Chalco in the eyes. The Indian seemed to hesitate. He pleaded with his eyes at Brannon and motioned with his head toward the leg.

Brannon stood and walked to the Indian.

"Surely you aren't going to assist in this savagery!" Fletcher groaned.

Brannon straddled the raised leg and nodded at Chalco. The Indian clamped down on the stick with his teeth and nodded back.

With split second quickness Brannon shoved Chalco's leg against the hot rock and barked out the words, "One-two-three-four-five!"

Chalco's face turned tight and red; tears rolled down his cheeks, but he didn't make a sound. Brannon pulled the leg up on the count of five, and he could smell the sickening aroma of burned flesh and blood. The Indian's face suddenly turned white, and his eyes rolled back. Chalco collapsed on the ground.

Brannon kicked the hot rock back into the fire circle and rejoined Fletcher.

"Good heavens, Brannon, you didn't kill him, did you?"

"I hope not. Just passed out, I suppose. It's tough taking a branding like that!"

"Was it really necessary for you to assist him?" Fletcher grimaced as he looked at the charred wound.

"Yep."

They were still standing and watching the unconscious Chalco when they heard the sound of a horse walking close behind them. Brannon whipped around and drew his Colt. Half expecting an ambush from Rutherford and men, he was surprised to see Red Shirt and Crazy Waters leading their horses towards the fire.

"The Brannon must have plenty bullets." Red

Shirt motioned towards the drawn gun.

"Red Shirt! We are glad to see you!"

"Good, I'm hungry," he replied helping himself to Chalco's plate of partially eaten food. Crazy Waters tethered their horses and rummaged for something to eat as well.

After several big bites of meat, Red Shirt pointed toward Chalco with his knife.

"Is he dead?"

"Nope."

"Did the Brannon shoot him?"

"Nope."

Red Shirt, still with a mouthful of food, smiled and nodded. "Good. Where is the man who shot Chalco?"

"Dead."

"Did the Brannon kill him?"

"Yep."

"Good."

"Why did Ouray send Chalco down here to trade when he couldn't speak the language?" Fletcher asked Red Shirt.

"Chalco brag a lot, and Ouray wanted to quiet him." Red Shirt looked over at the unconscious Ute and smiled. "It has worked."

Brannon motioned toward the supplies. "All of that is Chalco's."

"Very good!" Red Shirt grinned. "We will not be hungry for a while. Is the Brannon looking for more gold?"

"Not this time. We're headed to Arizona."

Red Shirt waved his arm toward the south.

"We will ride with you for part of the journey."

"Well," Brannon admitted, "we need to go back to Paradise Meadow first."

"We will wait." Red Shirt stepped over to examine Chalco's wounds.

"We will not be back until morning," Brannon cautioned.

"We will wait." He looked at the unconscious Ute. "Chalco does not feel well." Then he spoke in Ute to Crazy Waters who rose up and ambled over to pull their saddles off the horses.

"If we should happen to get delayed, you should go on," Brannon added.

"It will be our pleasure." Red Shirt helped himself to more hard tack.

Brannon and Fletcher waited until late in the afternoon before leaving camp.

"We can buy some supplies from Peter," Brannon suggested.

Chalco regained consciousness within a few minutes after Red Shirt's arrival and proceeded to describe in detail his ordeal including Creek, Fletcher, and Brannon's rescue.

"He says he is very grateful for your help," Red Shirt explained. "And he wanted to know about the woman. What tribe is she?"

"Tell Chalco she is the schoolteacher in Paradise Meadow. She is from the Cherokee tribe."

In excited Ute, Red Shirt and the others discussed the situation.

"I knew a Cherokee in Kansas once," Red Shirt reported. "He was smart man. Very smart man.

He taught English at the school. Women school-teachers? This is very, very delightful. Chalco said the woman is nicely beautiful, but that she only has eyes for the Brannon."

"What?" Brannon choked. "He said that?"

Red Shirt smiled broadly showing his full mouth of straight white teeth. "What happened to the woman in the blue dress who dug with you at the mine?" he asked.

"He must mean Velvet," Fletcher concluded.

"Well, she got married," Brannon reported.

Red Shirt told the others and then asked, "She married another man?"

"Yes, a very important man in the town of Tres Casas," Brannon replied.

After translating for the others, the three Indians broke out in uncontrollable laughter.

"I presume I'm the cause of all this." Brannon nodded at Fletcher.

"Quite."

Finally, turning to Brannon, Red Shirt explained, "Crazy Waters said you should have shot this important man for stealing your woman. And Chalco said maybe you wanted her stolen! He wishes someone would steal his woman!"

Red Shirt glanced at the other two and listened to their comments. Then he turned back to Brannon.

"Chalco says the Cherokee is much better looking. The lady in blue was too pale and white. He says the Brannon should carry off the Cherokee for his woman."

"Well, tell Chalco that the Cherokee is the kind of woman who would not let any man, white or Indian, carry her off."

"He says," Red Shirt continued, "that if you carry off the Cherokee, you are welcome to set up a tent in our camp. He is right. The Brannon would be welcome . . . with or without the Cherokee."

"Tell Chalco I am not going to town to see the Cherokee lady, and I have no intentions of carrying her off."

After a quick translation and discussion Red Shirt laughed. "He said you will change your mind!"

"Well, lady-killer," Fletcher said standing to his feet, "isn't it about time to ride?"

"Chalco said his leg is on fire, so I think we will stay here tomorrow also and rest. We will leave in two days."

"And we will be back tomorrow," Brannon insisted.

He and Fletcher resat their saddles and mounted up to ride back to town. Leaving Red Shirt and friends, they pushed their mounts up and into the forest of the western slope of the mountains.

The sun hung low and orange in the far distant west, and the trees cast long shadows as they plodded up the trail. Both men stopped and pulled on their coats, even though the evening breeze was mild.

"I trust we will have a little moonlight to assist

our journey," Fletcher offered.

"Edwin, this is the kind of night that makes you wish you were out on the range with a big herd of cows and calves!"

"Actually, I was thinking more of a walk in a garden with a lovely lady." Fletcher shrugged.

"You wouldn't have a particular lady in mind, would you?" Brannon teased.

"Lady Teresa Overton MacNeil," Fletcher admitted. "Did I ever tell you about the time —"

"No Lady MacNeil stories." Brannon laughed. "The last time you told those stories you went off to San Francisco and didn't come back for six weeks!"

At the base of a cliff they came out into a clearing.

"This meadow would be a nice place for a ranch headquarters." Brannon motioned. "Run them up the mountain in the summer and downhill in the winter. This is about in the middle. Put a corral along that cliff —"

"By the wagon wheel?" Fletcher nodded.

"Wagon wheel? I don't remember a wagon wheel when we came down." Brannon turned El Viento toward the cliff and trotted over to the wheel. Fletcher followed behind. A deep unseen barranca cut across the clearing near the base of the cliff.

"My word, Brannon, it's a whole wagon. There's been a wreck!"

Brannon was on his feet, running down the arroyo before Fletcher finished his sentence.

"Fletcher, give me a hand. It's Wishy . . . Wishy Boswick!"

"Good heavens, man . . . is he alive?"

"He's been shot in the head!" Brannon called. "I'll pull Wishy up. You see if you can coax this team to yank the wagon out! Wishy! Wishy? It's Brannon!"

The freighter opened one eye and stared.

There was a long pause as Boswick tried to focus.

"Just my luck," Wishy choked. "I get bushwhacked, and then the old boy who comes to rescue don't drink likker or chew tabacky. There are times when a man needs a good heathen friend!" He closed his eye.

"Hang on, Wishy, I'm carrying you out of this arroyo." Brannon pulled Boswick to his shoulders and struggled his way up out of the little canyon.

Laying Wishy back by some trees, Brannon brought his canteen off the saddle.

"Wishy, you've been partially scalped by that bullet. With that head wound you'll either live to be a hundred or die by morning."

"Brannon, you're a real comfort! They jumped me from the cliff, they did."

"Who did it, Wishy? It doesn't look like they tried to steal your rig."

"I suppose it was some of Rutherford's men." Wishy coughed.

"Why?"

"Well, it didn't help that I faced them down when they were giving Miss Rose a tough time."

"The teacher? She pulled you into this too?"

Wishy continued to talk, but closed his eyes. "Actually, I think Rutherford is trying to get rid of me and Mulroney."

"Peter? Did he get shot?"

"Shot? He's in jail for murder. Check my vest pocket. She sent you a note."

Brannon pulled Creek's note from the vest.

Dear Mr. Brannon,

Mr. Mulroney seems to think you are the only one who can help him avoid being hung for a murder he didn't commit. If you can be of assistance without shooting half the citizens of Paradise Meadow, please hurry back. Time is of utmost essence. The children are with me, and they have mythical trust in your ability.

Sincerely,
Rose Creek

Seems to think? Without shooting half the citizens? Mythical trust? She has quite a high view of you, Brannon.

Fletcher brought the team around, and they built up a fire close to Boswick. Digging into his supplies, they boiled some coffee and waited for the freight line owner to gain enough strength to explain the situation.

When Wishy finished describing Mulroney's di-

82

lemma, he ate a little bread and drank more water.

"Wishy, what's Rutherford's angle? I mean, I know he and his brothers were trying to steal someone's gold claim. But there's no gold right in Paradise Meadow, so what's he after? Being mayor can't make a man rich, can it?"

"Well, it hasn't hurt. The law in Paradise Meadow is you can't open a saloon without a liquor permit from the city."

"And Rutherford controls that?"

"Rumor has it that it will cost you five hundred cash dollars up front for the permit, and the mayor gets 25 percent of the take at all the saloons."

"Why doesn't someone do something about it?" Fletcher asked.

"Well, the prospectors don't care who owns the bar. And most of the owners are too busy rolling in the gold dust to complain. Besides, Rutherford has the gunmen . . . most of the rest of town is just shopkeepers, tradesmen, freighters, and the like."

"Wishy, can Mulroney get a fair trial in Paradise Meadow?"

"Fair trial? He won't even make trial. They'll hang him as soon as they can. Probably tomorrow, since you thwarted their other hangin'. They don't intend for that noose to just dally in the wind."

"Well, I've got to talk to Mulroney," Brannon reported. "So we'll just have to pull him out somehow. You said the old station serves as the jail?"

"Yeah, but the barn's gone."

"We noticed that. You doing all right? Can

we just leave you here for a while?"

"I'll either recover or die by daylight, so you said. Either way, I'm on my own. Go on, get Mulroney, but listen, Brannon, you've got to check on Miss Rose and the kids."

"Sean, Stephen, and Sarah?"

"Yep. They are stayin' with her. Rutherford and his cronies were treatin' her grievous poorly. If Mulroney escapes, she'll probably be the one to pay for it."

"Where are the townspeople? You mean to tell me there's not one man in town who'll stand by the schoolteacher?"

"They're all gold hungry and scared to death. Some good folks in there, Brannon, but they take fright easy, and they don't plan on staying long anyway."

"We'll be back by daylight." Brannon retrieved his big black horse.

"Look, Brannon, Rutherford will bluff easy, but he'll sneak around and shoot you in the back. Take a side trail out of town."

"Wishy, we got the fire built, coffee boiling, grub in the sack, and bullets in your gun. You're all set. What you need is some rest now. Keep your chin up . . . we'll be back."

"Yeah, Brannon, I reckon you will."

The clear Colorado night provided enough light to make out the trail ahead, but not much more. It was the kind of night when it's hard to discern a tree from a man. Brannon and Fletcher kept their horses at a fast walk as they climbed the mountain. The wind still whipped through the trees, and at times its roar prevented conversation.

"Do I have this right?" Fletcher probed. "The ex-sheriff of Tres Casas is going to break a man out of jail?"

"Yeah, I've been trying to justify it myself," Brannon admitted. "I know you can't bring order to a town by breaking laws, but there's no justice in Paradise Meadow."

"It's a risky pattern to establish," Fletcher offered.

"Yep. I suppose what I should do is take Mulroney up to Denver and turn him over to the marshal's office. That would force Rutherford to go up there and present his case."

"Of course, Rutherford wouldn't show up," Fletcher added.

"Nope. He just wants Mulroney out of town! That's why we're going back. According to Wishy, Rutherford appointed himself mayor . . . he sets the laws and enacts the sentences. There are some governments that need to be changed."

"Ah hah! Brannon, the political theorist!" Fletcher laughed. "Seriously, Stuart, how do we get Mulroney out of there? I mean, we know how difficult it is to saw through those logs."

"Then I suggest we walk through the door," replied Brannon. "The whole town will be asleep anyway."

After Wishy Boswick's departure, Rose Creek had decided to stay inside the rest of the afternoon. Realizing that Rutherford was not above an attack on women and children, she decided not to be an easy target.

Maybe I should have gone with Mr. Boswick. I don't have any right to keep putting these children's lives in danger. They deserve a safe, secure home.

Maybe Colorado was a mistake.

Maybe teaching was a mistake.

Maybe I should be tucked away in some reservation housing.

Maybe I —

"Miss Rose?" A voice from the street halted her bout of self-pity. "Miss Rose, are you in there?"

She started to pick up the shotgun, felt the stare of the children, then set it back down, and went to the door.

Jeremiah Gilmore stood on the sidewalk with a basket of groceries in his hand.

"Why, Jeremy, come in. The children are doing their lessons, but you won't disturb them."

"Miss Rose, I was at Fetterson's Mercantile, and they had this load of goods for you, but everybody was afraid to deliver them."

"Why is that, Jeremy?"

"You know, it's the mayor. He says nobody should help you 'cause you're an accomplice to murder."

"Then why doesn't he come arrest me?" she asked.

"There ain't . . . I mean, there isn't any more room in the jail. I heard him brag that by tomorrow night there would be plenty of room."

"You took a risk bringing these over," she cautioned.

"Yes, ma'am. I rightly expect I did."

"Listen, Jeremy, the folks over at the store haven't been too keen on selling me any supplies lately. How come they are sending these over?"

"I think some of them felt ashamed that you was the only one to stand up to Rutherford today — you and Brannon and his partner."

"Well, Mr. Brannon did seem to ride to town at the right time. Be sure and thank the folks over at the store." She smiled.

Jeremy Gilmore just stood and stared at her.

"Eh . . . Jeremy, is there anything else you wanted to say?"

"Ma'am? Oh . . ." he stammered, "listen, if you want me to, I could stick around and give you and the children some protection."

"Protection from whom?" She walked with him back to the front door.

"Miss Rose, I don't aim to scare you, but sometimes that Rutherford acts crazy."

"Thank you for your offer, but I think I can handle this myself." She nodded towards the shotgun.

"Well, listen, if you, you know, just happen to need a safe place, you can come out to Mr.

Miller's wagon. That's where I'm stayin'."

"You mean, Mr. Miller wouldn't mind my imposition?"

"He said if you wore your buckskins and let him take a picture, he wouldn't mind at all."

"I see. Well, Jeremy, I think I'll stay right here. But you can do me one favor."

"Yes, ma'am?"

"Just keep your eyes open around town. If they try to move Mr. Mulroney out of the jail, please let me know."

"You can count on it!" He grinned. "Miss Rose, that blue dress sure looks pretty on ya. It's a shame it got torn."

"Why, thank you, Jeremiah. Remember, if there's activity at the jail, you come let me know."

"Yes, ma'am!" He tipped his hat and left the school.

She thought she heard the children giggle. Then their voices faded, and she sat for several moments staring at the supply of groceries. Bread, cheese, eggs, a piece of fresh fruit, and some potatoes. But it wasn't the contents that held her attention. It was the thought that there were some other folks in Paradise Meadow who did not want to give in to Rutherford, some who wanted to support her in her efforts. It was the first sign of encouragement she had received since the mayor's Christmas speech.

She silently wept.

Right after dark she ventured out to the wooden

sidewalk in front of the schoolroom. The noise and congestion of the streets had slackened. The constant breeze had dried the street, and most of the freight wagons had started moving towards the mines further up.

Sarah stole out behind her.

"When's Daddy going to get out of jail, Miss Rose? Is Mr. Brannon really coming back? Did you know he is a Christian man? My mother said so. Are you a Christian, Miss Rose? Are you going to shoot someone with that shotgun? How come Jeremiah brought you a present?"

"Sarah, you have a lot of questions."

Sarah giggled.

"I don't have a lot of answers. I don't know the answers."

"Sometimes the answers are in the back of the book," Sarah offered.

If learning to live with other people were as easy as grammar and arithmetic! And if you could always find the answers in the back of the book!

"Sarah, you can't go to your place tonight, so you'll all stay with me in the schoolroom." They walked back into the building.

"Children, tonight we'll sleep with our clothes on. We might have to leave in a hurry, and I don't want us to have to take time to get dressed."

"Even our shoes?" Stephen questioned.

"No shoes or hats!" Creek joshed. "Don't worry. It will probably be a quite boring night."

FIVE

The shouts and shots of Paradise Meadow echoed through the trees long before the flickering lights of saloons and gambling parlors were visible under the star-filled Colorado night.

"Well, so much for a sleepy little village," Fletcher offered. "What now?"

Brannon reined up on El Viento and surveyed the reveling ahead of them.

"If we can't sneak up on them, we'll just ride straight at them. Chances are no one will recognize us in the dark. My guess is that they won't be expecting a visit."

Fletcher watched Brannon pull his revolver and spin the cylinder. "I say, Stuart, we aren't going to blast Mulroney out of jail, are we?"

"We'll both find out the answer to that soon enough. Let's tie the horses down by the creek and come up behind the cabin," Brannon suggested.

The street in front of the jail was part of the old freight line road from Tres Casas to the mines further up. It was officially named Camino Del Oro, but most often was called Del Oro Street. It was fairly straight, a little wider than the others, and was lined with saloons, cafes, and a hotel.

This night it was crowded with prospectors, would-be prospectors, gamblers, land agents, and dance hall girls. Pulling their hats low, Brannon and Fletcher joined the others milling in the street.

Stopping at a half-framed, tent-topped business that sported a sign, "Leroy's: Good Eating Is Done Here and Lots of It," Brannon plopped himself down on the wooden sidewalk and stared diagonally across the street at the log cabin jail that had once been the Broken Arrow Crossing stage station. He rested his Winchester across his knees.

Fletcher, squatting next to him, pushed back the front brim of his hat and brushed down his mustache with his fingers. "My word, Stuart, there is absolutely nothing about this place that seems familiar. It's like that whole hard winter was just a dream from the distant past."

"What I can't figure is how so many people with such meager shelter wintered out up here," Brannon commented.

"Or why," Fletcher added.

"The why is simple . . . gold fever will make the wise foolish, as we well know. Looks like they've got two men outside the jail."

"I suppose they could have more inside," Fletcher cautioned.

"True enough." Brannon nodded. "Let's find out!"

Suddenly he reached down and picked up a rock-hard dirt clod about the size of his fist. He hurled the clod through the night air, striking

91

the door of the cabin with a loud bang.

The two outside guards jumped to their feet with pistols drawn, but the busy street offered them no clues as to where the rock came from. A prospector staggered out of a place called Big Tilley's, fired two shots into the air, and stumbled back indoors.

The door of the jail opened, and a man stuck his head out. He said something to the two outside. Then he came out of the cabin and closed the door behind him. All three guards sat on a split log bench in front of the cabin.

"Well, we know there's three of them." Brannon nodded.

"Too bad there's not a back door," Fletcher said softly.

"Back door?" Brannon stood to his feet. "Fletcher, remember that hole we cut into the far wall so that we could pass between the barn and the cabin?"

"Certainly. But the barn burned down."

"But not the hole. They would have to fill it in. Maybe it's not all that secure."

"Well, it wouldn't be a good place to put a jail cell."

"Right. But it wouldn't hurt if it led into an office."

"And we could bring out Mulroney without those in front knowing it."

"That would be the plan."

"Just how do we carry it out?"

"I'll slip around the jail and check that old

crawl hole. The way they just left the ruins of the barn standing, I imagine they don't even know it's under those timbers."

"And what's my role?" Fletcher questioned.

"You watch from this angle. If any of the guards starts towards the cabin, stagger out into the street and fire off one round into the air. If they look like they're coming around to investigate the barn, fire off two shots."

"How are you going to tell my shots from some drunken miner's?"

"Because," Brannon said throwing his arm around Fletcher's shoulder, "you English have a funny accent!"

"Hey, you boys hungry? Why, come on in here and shovel down some of the best food in Paradise Meadow. We're still open, you know!"

Brannon turned to see a short man with a full beard spit tobacco juice at the road and then wipe his mouth on his dirty apron.

"Are you Leroy?" Brannon asked.

"Yep. You boys heard of me, have ya? Say, you two ain't never been down to Yuma, have ya?"

"No, I'm afraid not," Fletcher offered.

"Well, I'll be . . . he's a furiner, ain't he? It's O.K., all types is welcome in my establishment."

"That's a cheery thought." Fletcher smiled.

"I think we'll pass this time, Leroy, but thanks for the invite." Brannon nodded.

"You two ain't busted, is ya? God forbid that

a man goes hungry on my front steps. No, sir, I won't let no man starve. I'll stake you to a meal."

"Leroy, you're a generous man, but we have the funds." Brannon started to turn to Fletcher, then looked back at the cafe owner. "You can do us a favor. We're just passing through and need some supplies to take with us. I don't figure on waiting until a store opens up in the morning. How about fixin' us up a grub sack with coffee, bread, meat, and beans?"

"I got her. How much you boys need?"

Brannon flipped him a coin. "How about this much?"

"Mister, for a twenty-dollar gold piece I can feed you like Queen Victoria herself!"

"I say —"

"Relax, Edwin . . . that's a compliment. Just bring the supplies out here and give them to my funny-talkin' partner," Brannon teased.

"Yes, sir, I'll do that. Say, you boys like pickled eggs? You are going to have some of the best pickled eggs north of Magdalena!"

Leroy vanished back into his eatery as Brannon and Fletcher conferred.

"Are you set then?" Brannon asked.

"Quite." Fletcher sat down on the edge of the raised wooden sidewalk. "Brannon, do I sound that strange? I mean, really, I believe I've mastered this American dialect fairly stout!"

"Edwin, you blend in about like a white rabbit before the first snows hit. I'm going to check out that crawl space."

Brannon circled down toward the creek back behind the jail and came up to the old barn from the back side.

They just left it as it collapsed. It's a miracle that the fire didn't destroy the cabin.

Moving slowly and silently, he lifted the charred beams and timbers away from the end wall of the cabin. The general noise of Paradise Meadow's night life allowed him to work undetected in the dark. He located the place where the crawl hole was cut through the logs. As he expected, some boards had been nailed over the hole from the inside, but nothing had been done on the outside.

If I could kick that board, I could bust it, but not without stirring up those guards. A pry bar . . . I've got to find a pry bar.

Brannon spent the next few minutes in the dark on his hands and knees sorting through burned timbers trying to find a metal strap, iron bar, or plough shank — any scrap of metal. He found nothing but soot and ashes.

He dove flat into the beams when several men and horses rode up quickly to the front of the jail. He waited for Fletcher's warning shot, but heard none. Neither could he make out the conversation taking place in front of the cabin.

Returning to the crawl space, he laid on his back, pressed his boot heels against the boards that patched the hole, and grabbed on to the log wall. Applying pressure with his boots, he tried to force the nails to give way. Straining every muscle in his body, Brannon felt the board start to give. He rested a moment. As he did, he heard the mounted men ride off, this time towards the west.

Sounds like they picked up a few more riders.

Once again placing his boots on the boards, he strained to shove the patch off the crawl space hole. With one last groan he popped the nails out of the logs and sent the board sliding across the floor. Reaching around for his Winchester, he stuck his hands through the hole and then pulled himself halfway into the building.

Suddenly a match flickered near him, and candle light appeared, sprinkling faint light on the face of someone holding it.

"Peter, it's me — Brannon," he whispered.

A woman? "What is —"

"Don't cut him, Darrlyn, he's kind of cute, if his face weren't so dirty."

Next to the woman with the candle stood another woman in a brown dress that hung straight down about halfway between her knees and her ankles.

"Who . . ." Brannon tried to focus his eyes. One woman was holding a long thin knife.

"And I say we should stick him and then find out who he is!" she hissed.

"Darrlyn, I saw him first, and he's mine. You cain't stick him. Come on in, stranger. We'd be more hospitable, but this here's a jail."

Brannon kept his right hand on the trigger of

96

his rifle as he entered the jail. Standing upright he could look at both women at the same time.

Both wore brown dresses.

Both had matted, long blonde hair.

Both were young, not more than twenty.

Both had dirty faces.

Both had a fair complexion and blue eyes.

Both had flashing smiles.

And both smelled horrid.

"Twins?" Brannon choked. "You're twins?"

"What's the matter, ain't you never seen twins?" the one with the knife challenged.

"My sister's name is Darrlyn, and mine is Deedra, but you can call me darlin' anytime, sweetheart," the one with the candle whispered.

"Did you come to save us?" Darrlyn asked.

"Brannon! Stuart Brannon, is that you?" a male voice rasped out from the other side of the jail.

"Peter? Are you over there?"

"You're an answer to prayer, Brannon!" Mulroney called.

"Why, I should say so," Deedra cooed, "but how did ya'll know what we've been prayin'?"

"Peter, keep whispering, but tell me, what's the layout of this room?"

"There are two cells — the one you're in and the one I'm in. In between is a desk and a chair, a little office space, you might say."

"Yeah," Darrlyn said smiling, "you waltzed into the ladies' section. That's why this here sheet is hung up over the bar. We like our privacy!"

"Brannon, that's Deedra and Darrlyn Lazzard."

Brannon tipped his hat and nodded at the women.

"He's a gentleman, too," Deedra bubbled, "and he's mine!"

"Why are you ladies in here?" Brannon quizzed.

"For sticking a man with a six-inch blade," Deedra admitted.

"Only he couldn't identify which one of us did it," Darrlyn said, "so they locked us both up. He was an evil man."

"Ladies, I've got to get Mr. Mulroney out of that cell. Where are the keys?"

"Boise — he's one of the guards out front — he has one. And the mayor has one, and there's one in the desk." Darrlyn motioned.

"Peter, Fletcher's out front. We've got horses and we'll get you out of town."

"The children? Are they safe? Are they still with Miss Rose?"

"As far as I know, they are fine. Just keep still until I rescue those keys! Listen, eh, Darrlyn, hold that candle —"

"I'm Deedra," she corrected. "But you can call me darlin', or honey, or sugar."

"Look, Dee," Darrlyn snapped, "you're makin' a fool out of yourself. Mr. Brannon here is definitely not your type. He likes his women more refined and coy, like me," she insisted.

"You? You're about as refined as a rock quarry!"

"Listen, you dirty blonde huss—"

"Ladies!" Brannon hushed them. "Save it for later."

By holding on to the stock of his rifle, Brannon could reach through the iron bars of the cell and jam the nose of the octagon-barreled Winchester under the pull on the desk drawer. With several struggling tries, he was able to yank the drawer out about eight inches.

"There they are," Deedra whispered. "That's them on that brass ring, layin' on them papers."

"I can't reach them," he moaned. "I need a longer . . . eh, listen, Deedra —" he said to the twin with the knife.

"I'm Darrlyn. D-A-R-R-L-Y-N!"

"Right. Listen, Darrlyn, I need to borrow that knife. If I can lash it onto the end of the rifle, I might be able to reach those keys."

"No man ever took away my knife," she stated coldly.

"Well," Brannon paused, "I don't aim to take it away. I thought maybe you wouldn't mind me borrowing it while you combed your hair. Since you'll soon be out in public, I'm sure that you'll both want to fashion those beautiful golden locks of yours into something appropriately stylish."

"Well, now, he does talk, don't he?" Darrlyn smiled. She jabbed the knife towards Brannon and started to rummage around in the bunk behind her. "I don't care if you saw him first. He's not your type. I think he's a little sweet on me."

"You? Why I ought to —"

"Ladies! Shhh!" Brannon pulled a strip of rawhide off his holster and tied the knife to the barrel. On the first attempt he almost dropped the rifle. Several tries later the keys slid down the knife and gun into his hand.

Within moments he had unlocked the girls' cell, and then he crossed over and let Peter Mulroney out of his cell. Just as they moved toward the crawl space, suddenly the door of the cabin flung open. There stood Boise, Rutherford's hired man with his gun in hand.

"What the —" He started to raise his gun and then crumpled to the floor from a blow to the back of the head.

Fletcher, gun drawn and grub sack over his shoulder, stepped into the cabin and quickly closed the door. Brannon grabbed Boise by the boots and dragged him into Peter Mulroney's cell.

"Edwin?" Mulroney stammered.

"Women?" Fletcher choked.

"How about the others?" Brannon asked.

"They rode off with Rutherford." Fletcher stared at Deedra and then at Darrlyn.

"Twins," Brannon said.

"Well, ain't this a delicious sight. Three handsome men and only us two girls. Makes you want to throw a party now, don't it?" Deedra purred.

"One of them is purty dirty," Darrlyn added.

"I bet underneath all of that he's just purty!" Deedra eyed Brannon.

Ignoring the women, Brannon conferred with

Mulroney and Fletcher.

"Edwin, can we make it out the front?"

"I believe so. There is some commotion on the other side of town. No one seems to be concerned with what's happening over here at the moment."

"Look, we're going to circle around the cabin, cut down to the creek, and grab the horses. Peter, you ride on the big black with me. Then we'll head west —"

"How about us?" Deedra interrupted. "Do you have horses for us?"

"Ladies . . . look, you must have some friends here in town. So why don't you scoot over to their place and let them help you?" Brannon suggested.

"Oh, no you don't!" Darrlyn pouted. "Ain't no man goin' to dump me like that! You ask me to get all beautified and then send me home, no, sir, I won't stand for that. You'll have to treat me nicer than that. I'm going with you, Mr. Brannon."

"You ought to send her home, Stuart," Deedra whined. "I'm the one you really want to take with you! Besides," she insisted, "if you don't take me with you, I'll scream so loud it will wake up half the state of Colorado!"

"Look, eh, Miss Lazzards, if one of you stabbed a man, then you got to stand trial for that," Brannon reasoned.

"That won't work," Deedra answered.

"Why not?"

" 'Cause Loredo's dead now!" Darrlyn shrugged.

"You killed him?" gasped Fletcher.

"Nope. Mr. Mulroney killed him. So there's no one left to haul us to court."

"I didn't shoot anything but a kerosene lamp!" he protested.

"Wait," Darrlyn said with a sigh, "we was walkin' down the street mindin' our own business, and Loredo came out of the saloon and grabbed Deedra by the dress and yanked her back into the alley. I pulled my knife and told him to back off or I'd stick him. He jist laughed, so then I . . . I mean, so then one of us stuck him in the arm. He hollered like a pig and we ran off."

"Yeah," Deedra jumped in, "and they arrested both of us, but while they was trying to figure out which one did the stickin', the man got kilt in a gunfight with Mr. Mulroney. I sure do thank you, Mr. Mulroney. I think they was just keeping us in jail out of spite."

"I didn't kill him!" he insisted.

"Well, Mr. Law and Order," Fletcher queried Brannon, "what happens now?"

"For the time being, we'll just have to take them all with us."

"My word, are you serious?"

"Yep."

"Hey, are you from Australia?" Deedra asked Fletcher. "I once knew a man from Australia. A bank robber, I think he was."

"Good grief, no, I'm not from Australia!"

Fletcher protested.

"You got food in there?" Darrlyn pointed to the bag flung over Fletcher's shoulder. "They didn't give us no food today."

"What?" Brannon looked startled. "They didn't feed you?"

"Aye," Mulroney said, "and I don't think they were planning on us being in jail much longer."

"Fletcher, you lead them around the corner. Peter, you follow the ladies, and I'll come last. Are you ready?"

"Let's do it!" Fletcher peeked outside and then raced around the building.

Within a couple of minutes all five of them were out back leading the two horses and hiking up the bank of the creek. By staying on the outer edge of town they moved along unnoticed. As they got to the western road, they stopped to look at Paradise Meadow.

"Brannon," Mulroney confessed, "I can't leave the children with Miss Rose. They need to be with me."

"Look, we'll get you to safety and then slip back in town for the children," Brannon suggested.

"We will?" Fletcher groaned.

"Can't do it, Stuart," Mulroney repeated. "They've been through too much in the last week. I won't go off without them."

Brannon stared through the dark night at the Irishman.

"No . . . you're right. You can't leave them.

Well, Edwin, you stay here with the horses and the ladies. Peter and I will sneak back in. What with all that commotion over there, we'll hustle them out here in no time."

"Me? With the ladies? No, no, no . . . you stay with these, eh . . . ladies, and I'll go face a thousand angry gunmen!" Fletcher moaned.

"Sorry, old boy, I called it first!" Brannon chastened.

He pulled his extra pistol out of his gear bag tied behind the saddle and handed it to Mulroney.

"Peter, I don't expect you'll need this, but I've been wrong about just about everything in Paradise Meadow. Let's go get those children. Where's the schoolhouse?"

"Over by that disturbance, actually," he reported. "I hope they're not in danger."

"Miss Rose seems to be a capable woman," Brannon mumbled as he and Mulroney started out on foot.

Rose Creek bedded Sarah in her cot and tucked Sean and Stephen into pallets on the floor in the back of the schoolroom. Then she sat at the front of the room in the dark holding Wishy Boswick's loaded Greener shotgun across her lap. She purposely left it dark so as not to alarm the children by her posture.

It was not the first time in her life that she had held a gun to defend her position. But seven years previously she had pledged to herself and her friends that she would use reason, not violence, to solve problems.

Well, Rose, you really made it big. You live in fear. Every dress you own is torn and dirty. You endanger the lives of children. You hate most men. And you don't trust God anymore. Can't get much more miserable than that!

She laid the shotgun aside and walked back to check on the children. Finding them asleep, she lit a small lantern and carried it over to her trunk. Opening the chest, she reached in for her sewing basket. As she did, she glanced at the beaded buckskin dress that lay in the bottom of the trunk.

I should wear that dress! It's certainly better for a fight. I ought to pull on moccasins, stick my knife in the sheath, braid my hair, and wear the buckskins. If they want to fight Indians, then I'll give them an Indian.

Instead, she closed the trunk and slipped off the blue dress to mend it. Once she finished that job, she poured herself a basin of water and washed her face and arms. Having pulled the dress back on, she strained in the flickering light to look in the mirror and comb her long black hair. Rather than retie it up behind her head, she pulled her hair back off her shoulders and clipped it with a mother-of-pearl comb.

I am a schoolteacher of Indian descent. They will not make me act like anything else.

She had just turned off the lantern and resettled in the chair up front when she heard noise on the street in front of the school. The canvas-walled building allowed her to hear everything.

"Hey, half-breed! Are you in there? Listen, the mayor has declared that Paradise Meadow is off limits to Injuns. You hear me? We come to clear you out. We don't want no trouble. You jist grab your things, and we'll escort ya out of town. There don't got to be trouble here; you jist come along!"

She picked up the shotgun, checked for shells in both barrels, and remained silent.

"She's in there! I know she's in there!"

"We could set the whole place on fire. That would send her out!"

"Cain't do that . . . them kids is in there too!"

"Them kids is as good as orphans anyway!"

"Let's go in there and drag her out," a third voice suggested.

"Rutherford said not to stir up the neighbors!"

"Well, we ain't gettin' nowhere this way."

"Then you go in and grab her."

"I ain't goin' through that door alone."

"Come on, we're all going in!"

Rose's shout woke the children.

"The first one of you derelicts that comes into this schoolroom gets a shotgun blast to the midsection. The second one gets the other barrel. I'd suggest those of you who desire a long life to hang towards the back of the mob!" she called.

"She's bluffin'," she heard one say.

"I ain't goin' to find out."

"You go in there, Thrush!"

106

"Not me . . . no, sir!"

Suddenly, there was chaos in front of the tent and at the back at the same time. She heard a new voice.

"You men go on back to the saloon where you belong. You can just leave our schoolteacher alone."

Is that Mr. Fetterson? Did he say "our" schoolteacher?

"Well, look who has a pistol in his hand. You sure you know how to use that, storekeep?"

"Why, he's quite a brave man. Probably did this to impress the little wife. Well, you jist trot home and tell her how courageous you were, and maybe we'll let you live one more day."

"Or maybe we'll shoot you in the back!"

"I'm warnin' you men!" Fetterson shouted.

"Miss Rose," Sarah called, "someone's cutting a hole in the canvas."

Creek, carrying the shotgun, hurried to the back.

"Sarah, get your shoes on, and tell your brothers to do the same!" she commanded.

"Miss Creek?" a woman's voice called.

"What do you want?"

"Miss Creek, I'm Mrs. Fetterson. Please, you and the children come with me! We must hurry!"

"Sean! Stephen! Sarah! Come on!" Rose commanded. She could no longer distinguish words in the shouts of voices from the front street.

They climbed up on a chair and through the slit canvas. Mrs. Fetterson and an older woman helped them to the ground.

"My Henry is trying to keep them distracted out front. We must hurry back to the store!"

"Your Henry is a very brave man!"

"He is not brave, maybe foolish, in fact, but he is very tired of being afraid of Rutherford."

The women and children ran through the night past rows of tents and across the open floors of partially framed buildings. Fetterson's Mercantile was one of the few finished buildings in town.

In the flight . . . in the dark . . . in the mud and dirt streets of Paradise Meadow, Colorado . . . amid the fear . . . out of breath . . . with feet aching . . . and little Sarah's hand clutched tightly in hers . . . Rose Creek, for the first time, felt she was not alone in wanting to tame an uncivilized land.

SIX

A dark night can make brave men cowards. It can also make cowards brave. It can cause wise men to act foolish.

But it seldom causes foolish men to act wise.

When Brannon and Mulroney approached the clash of men and flickering lanterns in front of the school, the street was filled with the brave, the foolish, and the cowardly.

In the shadows of Paradise Meadow it was difficult to tell the difference.

The two walked straight up to the confrontation. Crowded around the narrow winding street were about two dozen people — mostly men, a few women . . . some in night clothes . . . several with all winter's dirt and grime still on their shirts . . . some carrying weapons . . . some carrying lanterns . . . all stood watching a fight take place in front of the school.

It wasn't much of a fight. Six hard-looking men were beating a small man senseless.

Some in the crowd complained.

A few cheered.

Most merely watched.

"Peter, who is that? They're going to kill him!"

"It's Henry Fetterson. Owns that big Mercantile," the Irishman offered. "What's he doing

109

going up against Rutherford's hired guns?"

"He's getting busted in two. He won't have one bone left that's not broken," Brannon replied. "Where does this crowd stand? Are they all Rutherford's men?"

"No . . . mostly good folks, but they won't face down this gang."

"Peter, I'll make the first move. You hang back and see that none of them pulls a gun on my back. But try not to start shooting. When bullets go flying, innocent folks can get hurt."

"What are you going to do?"

"Save a man's life, I hope!"

Those attacking Fetterson hardly saw Brannon dash into their midst. He charged in low, smashing the barrel of his rifle into the knees of a man kicking Fetterson. The man fell, screaming in pain.

Then Brannon stood up quickly, jerking the butt of the rifle into the chin of another man, crumpling him to the dirt. At the same time he hammered the barrel of the Winchester alongside the head of the third man, dropping him. Spinning, he brought the rifle within two inches of the man called Cleve.

"Tell those other two to drop their guns!" Brannon shouted.

Totally surprised, Cleve stammered, "Drop 'em, boys . . . drop 'em! It's Brannon!"

Jamming the rifle under Cleve's chin, Brannon almost lifted him off the ground.

"What are you doing, trying to blow out

Fetterson's lamp?" he barked.

"This man drew a gun on us, and we were merely trying to disarm him!" Cleve explained.

"Disarm him? You were about to dismember him!"

"Brannon, this ain't none of your business!"

"Whose business is it then to see that the people of this community don't get beat to death? Where's your town marshal?"

"Well . . . ya jist about plumb broke his legs in two . . . he's the one over there hollerin'."

"The marshal? Kicking a helpless man? Did anyone in the crowd see how this got started?"

No one answered.

Brannon looked over at a man and woman who had come outside in their night clothes. "Mister, I don't know you, but I want you and your wife to get over there and help Mr. Fetterson. When he's able to talk, we'll find out what happened."

They moved over to Fetterson.

"You folks live nearby?"

"Yes, sir." The man pointed. "Right over there."

"Then you take Mr. Fetterson to your place and clean him up a bit. Would you do that for me?"

"Uh . . . yes, sir, we will."

"Brannon!" Mulroney yelled.

One of the gunmen behind Brannon stooped to grab his pistol, and Brannon whipped around to see Peter Mulroney catch the man under the chin with his knee. As the man's head snapped backward, Mulroney brought the barrel of the pistol down across the man's head dropping him cold.

The remaining gang member caught Mulroney with a wild roundhouse and sent the Irishman stumbling. Brannon stepped forward to stop the attack, and Cleve made a break for the darkness and the tent buildings.

Brannon saw Mulroney bounce to his feet and hit the man with three bone-crushing right jabs and a left uppercut. Stuart turned to chase Cleve through the night.

It was a hopeless pursuit. Darkness and the scrambling crowd erased all hope of success. Brannon spun around to see Mulroney deck the man with two more powerful punches.

"Peter, you should be a boxer," Brannon called out.

"I am." He reached down to pick up his hat. "Where's the other one?"

"Got away. We need to act fast," Brannon ordered. "He'll drag Rutherford and others back here. Go get Miss Rose and the children, quickly!"

The crowd still milled around in front of the schoolhouse.

"Look," Brannon called, "I don't know where you all stand in this scrape, but Rutherford himself and the others will be scootin' over here any minute. I'd suggest you get out of the street because they're going to be powerful mad."

"They was threatenin' Miss Rose," one of them

spouted. "That ain't right . . . even if she is a breed."

"I heard it too," another voice shouted.

"Somebody should've stopped them earlier."

"They deserved what they got after beatin' up on Mr. Fetterson. That man never hurt nobody in this town! Why, he helped ever' one of us git through the winter."

"Well, you make sure you tell him that! There's not one man in a thousand will do what he just did."

"Brannon!" Mulroney yelled. "Nobody's in here!"

"Mr. Brannon! Mr. Brannon!" a young man's voice called out. "Over here, Mr. Brannon!"

Brannon eased his way into the dark with his hand still clutching his Winchester.

"Mr. Brannon —"

"Do I know you?"

"Jeremiah Gilmore. I met you last fall up at the mine. I'm the assistant to Hawthorne Miller."

"The photographer and pulp novelist?"

"Yeah . . . listen," he huffed, "I saw you break Mr. Mulroney and the others out of jail. So I was coming over to tell Miss Rose, like I promised her, but she and those children escaped out the back of the school. Some women helped her."

"Where did they go?" Mulroney prodded.

"I don't know. I saw you two come into this crowd, and I waited to see what would happen. I think maybe one of the women was Mrs. Fetterson."

"Perhaps they went to the Mercantile!" Mulroney suggested.

"I'll come help ya," Jeremiah offered.

"Jeremy, if you want to help, stay here and figure out what Rutherford's up to next."

"Where will I meet you?"

"I'll find you. Where you staying?"

"At the wagon on the other side of the creek."

"If I need your help, I'll meet you there. Now hang back in the crowd and don't get yourself hurt."

Brannon and Mulroney raced through the dark, winding paths and streets to Fetterson's Mercantile.

"Can you trust the lad?" Mulroney asked.

"Jeremiah? Well, he's at that age between hay and grass. Seems to be a friend of Miss Rose. My guess is that he's on the square."

The store was shuttered tight, but Brannon could see a little lantern light filter under the door. He banged on the outer door.

"Mrs. Fetterson! Open up!"

There was no answer.

"You try it, Peter. Maybe they'll recognize your voice."

"Miss Rose? Are you in there, Miss Rose? This is Peter Mulroney!"

A little voice echoed out to the two men standing on the wooden sidewalk.

"That's Daddy!"

"It's my Sarah." Mulroney smiled. He pounded on the door again.

Slowly the door cracked, and Mrs. Fetterson appeared, carrying a lantern in one hand and a pistol in the other. She smiled at Peter Mulroney and then lost the smile when she saw Brannon. For a moment she didn't move.

"Mrs. Fetterson?" Mulroney spoke quickly. "This is Stuart Brannon. He helped me escape and just laid out that whole gang that was whippin' on Mr. Fetterson."

"Oh, my! Come in . . . excuse me. Is Henry all right? Did they kill him?" she stammered trying to breathe deeply and steel herself for the worst.

"No, ma'am, he's not dead. But he is pretty well beat up."

"Where is he?"

"With some neighbors, I believe," Brannon replied as he stepped inside and closed both doors behind him.

"He's with the Highsmiths," Mulroney explained. Suddenly the Irishman was mobbed by Sean, Sarah, and Stephen.

Brannon just stared for a moment.

"Peter, you're a rich man." Brannon pushed back his hat and blinked back moisture in his eyes.

"Mr. Brannon! Do you normally fight your way into every town?" Rose Creek stepped into the lantern light.

"Eh . . . well, I can see your opinion of me has remained constant," he managed to mumble.

"Mr. Brannon!" Stephen ran over and grabbed

115

him around the leg. "Did you really find gold up there? Is that my money that you told Miss Rose about? Did you shoot a man dead out in the forest? Are you going to be the marshal of Paradise Meadow?"

"Stephen," Brannon said smiling, "I'm really glad to see you and Sean and Sarah! I'm not going to be marshal, but most of the rest is true." Then he turned to Peter Mulroney.

"We've got to get you and the children and Miss Rose out of town."

"You're all leaving town?" Mrs. Fetterson asked.

"Well, ma'am, we've got to get Peter to a safe spot until this matter about a man's death can be settled. Miss Rose, I think it would be best for you to leave too."

"I'm not deserting my school!" she insisted.

"I don't want you to desert it," Brannon replied. "Just move it to a different location until the students' safety can be assured. You've got to think of the children."

She flipped back her long black hair over her shoulder and glanced at the floor. Then she tilted her head, looked Brannon in the eyes, and sighed.

"You're right, of course. Where are we going?"

"Tres Casas."

"New Mexico?"

"Yep. It's the closest place where I can guarantee safety. Rutherford won't go down there."

"How will we get there?" she asked.

"We'll have to walk a few miles. Then Mr.

116

Boswick has a wagon," Brannon reported.

She turned to Mulroney. "I'm afraid I didn't have a chance to pick up many of the children's belongings. All we have is what we have on."

"Ma'am, there's nothing on this earth that can't be replaced . . . except for you and these children. I just can't thank you enough. I'm sure there are rewards in Heaven for folks like you, Miss Rose." Mulroney buttoned Sarah's coat and grabbed Stephen's hand. "Brannon, we'd better get moving!"

Brannon cracked the doors and peered out into the darkness. Then he turned back to Mrs. Fetterson.

"Ma'am, will you be safe?"

"I believe so. I wish you'd brought Henry back."

"I should have. I was distracted by Rutherford's men and just wanted to get him off the street. I imagine the neighbors will bring him home any minute now. Do you have any help around here?"

"You mean employees? Yes, of course, but they won't be in until 7:00 A.M."

"Look, I can stay if you need some protection," he offered.

"Mr. Brannon," Miss Rose spoke up, "it just might be they would be safer if you weren't around. You don't exactly inspire good behavior in Rutherford and his men."

"Mrs. Fetterson?" Brannon raised his eyebrows.

"Well . . . Miss Rose might be right. But that

means they'll try to track you down!" she cautioned.

"Once we get to the woods, they'd be fools to follow us until daylight. You keep this door bolted until you know for sure who's there."

"I certainly will."

"Brannon, I hear some noise over by the school!" Mulroney shouted.

"Peter, grab the boys. Miss Rose, hold on to Sarah. I'll carry that shotgun. Good-bye, ma'am, you take good care of your Henry. It's men like him who will make the West a fit place for families to live."

The shouts in the distance seemed to be more of a harangue than an argument as Brannon and the others hurried through the night. Mulroney and the boys led the way. Then came Sarah and Miss Rose. Brannon put himself between the others and any chance of an attack.

The streets and paths of Paradise Meadow were mostly dry. The night breeze still blew stiffly from the west, and the stars just offered enough light for them to keep from tripping over tent pegs and wagon ruts. Seeing no sign of attempts to follow them, Brannon watched Rose Creek as she scurried up ahead with Sarah.

Quick . . . strong . . . opinionated . . . talk about a fighter. Three women like her could tame almost any town in the West. She's a stander. You'd have to kill her to stop her. Probably tough enough to take on the Arizona desert, the Apaches, and . . .

Brannon, this is the stupidest conversation with

yourself you've ever had.

On the other hand, she is quite a beautiful woman.

"Peter! Over this way," Brannon called. He took the lead and brought them into the trees just past the hanging log and next to the western road.

"Edwin?" he called.

"Over here. My word, you found the children. And the schoolteacher! How splendid. Actually, I don't believe we had time for introductions before. I'm Edwin Fletcher." He tipped his hat at Miss Rose.

She nodded while everyone huddled in the dark near Brannon.

"Where are the twins?" Brannon asked.

"Twins? The — the Lazzards?" Miss Rose stuttered. "You brought them with you? Why? Or should I not ask with children present?"

"We brought them," Fletcher insisted, "because we could not get rid of them. They developed quite an attraction for Stuart."

"Where did you say they were?" Brannon asked again.

"Over by the horses."

"I don't hear them."

"Precisely. You have me to thank for that," Fletcher added.

"But . . . how?"

"I gagged and tied them."

"You what?"

"Look for yourself. They began to scream at each other over who had the biggest piece of *carne asada.* When they started pulling hair, I tied and gagged them."

"Edwin, I'm impressed. I wouldn't have believed one man could have done it." Brannon smiled.

"It was not without cost." The Englishman grimaced. "I've got scratches in the back of my neck that are still bleeding and a bite in my leg."

"Well . . . we've calved 'round long enough. Untie them and let's get down the mountain to Wishy's camp. Then we can load up everyone in the wagon and put some miles between us and Paradise Meadow."

"Untie them? You must be joking," Fletcher groaned. "You untie them."

Brannon began to give orders.

"Peter, mount Stephen and Sean on Fletcher's sorrel. You can lead it. Miss Rose, you and Sarah ride El Viento. I know you have on a dress . . . and a pretty dress at that, but can you fork a horse in it?"

"I'm quite able to walk," she insisted.

"I can see that, ma'am . . . but El Viento is a might spirited, and I can tell you've spent some time on the back of a pony, so it would be of help to little Sarah to have you mounted."

Creek whipped around and looked Brannon in the eyes. "You can tell I've ridden horses by looking at me?"

"Yes, ma'am, you see I've studied you and I —"

"You've studied me? You've studied me!" she snapped. "Am I a botanical specimen to be kept in a glass jar and 'studied'?"

"Miss Rose . . . if you don't get on that horse, Sarah is going to have to walk."

Brannon turned away from the others and went to untie the twins. Fletcher had them bound back to back. Now they looked mad enough to bite the rope in two.

He paused, pushed back his hat, and sighed.

"Ladies, listen to me carefully. We're going to travel through the night as silently and quickly as possible. There isn't any time for mean-spirited arguments or even friendly discussions. Do you understand?"

They nodded their heads.

"You promise there will be no fights or yelling?"

Again they nodded their heads. Having untied them, he removed the gags.

"That thar Australian had no business tying us up! Is he a convict? I heard all them Australians is convicts!"

"I am not Australian!" Fletcher boomed through the night.

"Ladies, you'll have to walk until we get to the wagon," Brannon announced.

One of the twins grabbed Brannon's arm. "I'll be happy to walk by your side," she purred.

"Listen, Deedra, you and your sis—"

"Just call me darlin'," she broke in.

"She ain't Darrlyn. I'm Darrlyn." Her sister grabbed Brannon's other arm.

"I'm his darlin', ain't I, Stuart?"

"Neither of you is my darlin'!" He tried to shake off the girls' grip.

"Maybe he's sweet on the schoolteacher in her fofarraw dress!" Darrlyn suggested.

"Oh, no, let me assure you . . . eh, ladies," Miss Rose called out, "Mr. Brannon is definitely not my type. So you two are quite free to continue to embarrass yourselves by your childish behavior."

Suddenly the twins dropped Brannon's arms and walked on off ahead of the horses.

"Thanks." Brannon nodded at Miss Rose.

"You certainly didn't look like you were in pain," she added.

Brannon sent Fletcher in the lead holding El Viento's headstall. Sarah and Miss Rose straddled the big black. Creek carried Boswick's Greener shotgun. Peter Mulroney led the sorrel, with Stephen and Sean riding. Darrlyn and Deedra surprised everyone by keeping quiet. They trailed along and chewed on the jerky that had been the cause of an earlier argument.

The pace was slow, and Brannon was fairly sure Rutherford and some of his gang would try to follow them. The road switch-backed up the mountain, crested in the pine ridge, and then began the *bajada* towards the canyon country.

At each turn he could look between the trees and see a few flickering lights of the town. He figured that there were about three more hours before daylight, and he wanted to make it to Boswick's wagon by then.

Hiking up the wagon road, staring out into the dark night, Brannon thought of Arizona. *Lord, it's time to go home. I want to settle down in that ranch house . . . raise some cows . . . break some colts . . . put on a boiled shirt and ride to church on Sundays. I want to have time to read and write some letters . . . and sit out on the veranda and doze off. Give those folks in Paradise Meadow the courage to do the right things . . . and give us wisdom as we go on down the road —*

"Brannon! I say, Brannon!"

He looked up, startled, as Fletcher and the others hesitated in the trail and stared back through the night at Paradise Meadow.

"That looks like a fire!" Creek pointed the Greener through the dark Colorado night.

"What is there in town that could burn?" Fletcher asked.

"With this breeze, the whole town could be gone by morning!" Brannon strained to see more clearly down the hillside.

"The school . . . would they burn down the school?" Then Miss Rose answered her own question. "They would, wouldn't they?"

"Or Fetterson's store maybe," Brannon offered. "I didn't like leaving her alone. Look, I'm going back. Fletcher, you and Mulroney take the rest on to Wishy's camp. When you get there, I need you —"

"I say, Brannon, you can't go back in there alone! I'll go with you."

"No! I said, you go ahead. Look, if Wishy's

still alive, you need to get him down to Doc Shepherd at Tres Casas. Peter and these children must travel as far from Paradise Meadow as possible."

"Mr. Brannon," Sarah called out, "me and Miss Rose can walk. You'll need your horse!"

He glanced at Creek.

"I'm sure Sarah can keep up with the others." She slid off El Viento and helped Sarah down.

"We're going with you, darlin'," Deedra whined.

"Ladies, I wouldn't dream of exposing you to such danger," he mumbled.

"Well," Deedra sighed, "he is dreamin' about us after all!"

Darrlyn pulled out her knife and came over by Brannon. "You will need some help. Me and Dee do have experience with them boys of Rutherford's." She grinned.

"If you ladies want to really impress me, here's what you do. You help get these children to safety. Then you go to the Davis & Wendell Hotel in Tres Casas. You get yourselves a nice room, a hot bath . . . no, two hot baths. Then you go out and buy a couple of calicoes . . . maybe ribbons for your hair. That way when I make it to town and want to take you to dinner, I'll be the envy of every man in New Mexico."

"I knew it," Darrlyn drawled, "he's sweet on me. I just knew from the time we met."

"You?" Deedra shouted. "The only reason he invited you to dinner was that he's afraid your feelin's would get hurt. It's me he's after!"

"Ladies! Can I count on you to help the others get to Tres Casas?"

"For you, darlin', I'd hike all the way to the Boston Commons so we could be married at the Old Church!" Deedra grabbed his arm and tried to kiss him on the cheek.

Brannon pulled back and bumped right into Darrlyn kissing the other cheek.

"Ya know," Darrlyn crooned, "if you was Mormon, you could marry us both!"

"Well, if you three are quite finished," Miss Rose interrupted, "I think it's time to move out. Sarah, go up there and hold your daddy's hand."

"I can walk with you, Miss Rose."

"No, honey, I'm going back to town. I need to help those folks too."

"Now look, Miss Creek," Brannon started, "there's no way I'll —"

"Mr. Brannon, I did not ask you for permission to return. Nor do I need to. You can buffalo, hornswoggle, and sweet-talk the others, but not me."

"I don't have time to argue; it's too dangerous!" He grabbed the horn and pulled himself aboard El Viento.

"Give me your hand, Mr. Brannon," she commanded. He hesitated.

"Look, as a people we've been run out of almost every square mile in this country. There's not a town I can go to in the West where my life isn't in some danger. Well, don't ask me why

125

I ended up at the edge of the earth in a place like Paradise Meadow . . . but I did! And I've drawn the line. I'm not going to be run out of town by guns, or men, or fear. When I leave, it will be on my own terms and at a time I decide. Now give me your hand!"

She still held Boswick's Greener as he leaned over and pulled her up behind him on El Viento.

"I say —" Fletcher protested.

"Get them all to Tres Casas and send word to the U.S. Marshal's office up at Denver. They need to send some men in here, or there won't be a soul left standing. Then high-tail it back up here and bring a little extra ammunition."

"Do you know what you're doing?" Fletcher questioned.

"Edwin, I haven't known what I was doing for two years! Now go on!" He spurred El Viento, and they turned and trotted off into the night.

Rose Creek sat sidesaddle atop Brannon's sougan, which was rolled tight against the cantle. He held her shotgun, along with his Winchester, across his lap. Even though he had slowed his horse, the strong wind whipped her long black hair, which she hadn't had time to pin up or bonnet. Her arms were clamped around Brannon's waist, a pose she didn't relish, but it was the only way she knew to keep from tumbling to the roadway.

Yesterday I wouldn't have gone back. Yesterday the Mulroney children didn't need me. Yesterday

126

no one in this town seemed to care whether I was here or not. Yesterday no one stood out in front of the school and took a beating that had probably been meant for me.

And yesterday I had never met Stuart Brannon!

He reminds me of . . . of Jimmy Swiftcurrent.

For a moment, Rose was only thirteen, riding the wind on a paint horse through the green hills of springtime on the Indian Nation. Racing alongside of her on a long-legged bay was Jimmy Swiftcurrent. He would always win the race. He could shoot straighter, run faster, and outride her. But, just barely.

Most of the time she couldn't remember if she hated Jimmy or liked him. He could make her mad enough to scream. He could make her laugh for hours at a time. He would tell her all about his girlfriends and would chide her because she had no boyfriend.

I had a boyfriend!

Jimmy, you didn't have to race them! It was stupid. You told me it was stupid. They were bad men. They were hiding from the law! Why did you have to go down there!

Rose cried for seven days after Jimmy was murdered. On the eighth day, she enrolled in Fem Sem.

Only fools like the twins could love a man like Brannon. He will not live long enough to get to know well, let alone to love. You will not occupy my thoughts, Mr. Stuart Brannon.

But she did have to admit, it felt good to hold on tight to a strong man.

Brannon's thoughts bounced as El Viento rounded each corner and jumped the wagon ruts.

Not her type? I don't know why she thought she was even under consideration. I mean, at least I can understand the twins. Their intentions are obvious. Lord, I really don't need any more complications.

She's a lot like Lisa though. Dark hair . . . flashing eyes . . . wide, easy smile. And stubborn. Maybe tougher.

The desert was harsh on Lisa. I should never have taken her out there. If we had been near town, if we had lived in Prescott, she and the baby could still be alive! If I didn't have this fool idea about a cattle ranch. Maybe a feed store, or blacksmithing. I could at least marshal . . . Lord, You know I had to be on that ranch. I told her that before we were married. Lord, I tried to scare her off! Why didn't she listen?

El Viento stumbled and then righted himself. Rose clutched even tighter to Brannon. The warm touch of a woman brought his mind back to the present.

She could make it out on a ranch. She's got grit. She wouldn't slow a man down. She'd pull her share. She's insulted if I think she can't handle something on her own. Well, I'll treat her like she wants. She deserves a chance to prove herself. She's not a squaw, not a breed . . . just a lady who needs

some folks to give her a chance. Lord, she deserves
that much.

They pulled up to the edge of town and could
see the flames lap the sky on the far side of
town near the creek.

Brannon turned back and spoke rapidly.

"Miss Rose, it doesn't matter if you're full-
blooded or a half-breed, whether you were Irish
or Italian, whether you were born in a mansion
or teepee, whether your father is a chief or a
horse thief. I will treat you the same. But I will
not treat you like a man. I only know how to
treat you one way, and that is like a lady."

She stared for a moment as if she hadn't heard
him.

He could see the faint lights of Paradise Meadow
twinkle in her eyes.

"And, Mr. Stuart Brannon," she replied, "I
will not cry seven days for you if you die."

SEVEN

For a moment Stuart Brannon could feel that warm morning breeze off the Arizona desert.

And Rose Creek could smell the green spring grass along the North Canadian river.

An explosion from the far side of Paradise Meadow spun their minds in another direction.

"Are they shooting?" Creek questioned.

"Maybe," Brannon answered. "It sounded more like some black powder . . . maybe dynamite. Must be plenty of it stashed around here waiting to get to the mines. The way it's burning I think it's the jail that caught fire. It's the only building of much substance over there, isn't it?"

"Yes . . . but the jail? Rutherford wouldn't burn down his own jail!"

"Maybe someone got mad at him," Brannon suggested.

"No one in this town would dare stand up to him."

"Fetterson did."

He saw Creek lower her eyes at the mention of Fetterson. "Even so, why would anyone burn down the jail?"

"I suppose it could be by accident. You know, a busted lantern or something. Or then, it could be a diversion." Brannon offered.

"Diversion?"

"Maybe they're going to try something over on this side of town. That would sure be a good way to get everyone's attention elsewhere."

Creek glanced at Brannon. "You mean . . . like the school?"

"Or maybe Fetterson's!" Brannon handed her the Greener. "Presume you know how to use this?"

"In my wilder days, I pulled off a round or two," she admitted.

"Wilder? Poised and proper Miss Rose Creek?"

He met a warning scowl, so he started walking the horse through the dark twisted lanes and streets of Paradise Meadow in the general direction of the school.

"Rutherford won't be too happy with your return."

"Nope." Brannon tugged his black hat lower in the front.

"I expect there will be trouble," she said softly.

"Yep."

"What is there that attracts you to trouble, Mr. Brannon?"

"What?"

"I'm a Cherokee woman. Hard times seem to follow me around. So I'm used to it by now. But you . . . you actually delight in jumping into the midst of the most potentially violent situations. Why?"

"Habit."

"Stuart Brannon, you . . . you use one-word answers to try and get me to stop asking personal questions, don't you?"

"Yep."

"Well, it won't work on me. Is there some thrill in the violence or what?"

"Nope. Listen, I honestly don't always know why I do what I do. I guess I feel like things should be done right and people treated fair. And . . ."

"And what?"

"I've acquired a few skills in handling a gun, an extra dose of common sense, respect for the Almighty, and have very little to worry about. Surprising how brave a man can be when he's got nothing to lose."

They squeezed between two freight wagons and turned down a narrow twisting street.

"No!" she gasped. "Is that the school?"

Even in the near dark of night, they could see that the center support posts and ceiling trusses had been pulled down and the roof collapsed on the building. School supplies and Creek's personal belongings littered the street.

"No!" she cried, slipping down off El Viento. "Not the schoolroom! We had so little . . . not the chalkboard . . . our readers! They just threw our books out into the street! It took me three months to get these readers sent up!"

"It looks like they trampled right over everything." Brannon dismounted and tied the horse to the handle of a trunk that littered the road

132

in front of the school.

"What kind of men are they?" she cried. "Sneaking around in the dark attacking women, children, and schoolrooms?" Frantically, she began to scurry through the now silent streets and scoop up slates and supplies.

"Miss Rose? . . . Rose!" Brannon yelled.

She stopped and stood up, blankly staring at Brannon.

He grabbed her shoulders. "Rose! Listen, we've got to check on the Fettersons. We can come back after daylight and clean up here. Do you understand?"

"They tore up my trunk." She walked over to El Viento. "Everything I owned in the world was in that trunk!" She glanced inside the crushed wardrobe. "Where are my buckskins? I can't believe they would take my buckskins!"

"Rose? Are you all right?"

She reached up to wipe her eyes.

"Mr. Brannon . . . someone's going to pay. This will cost him dearly!" she promised.

"Come on." He took the reins of El Viento and began to sprint towards Fetterson's Mercantile, pulling the horse. He quickly looked back. Rose Creek neatly stacked several books in front of the rubble of the schoolroom, picked up the shotgun, and then scurried to catch up.

The tall, rough-cut false front of the Mercantile stood like a monolith in a sea of tent-top buildings. It was quiet, and the doors and windows remained shuttered, just as they had been earlier in the evening.

"Well, at least they didn't do anything over here." Creek motioned.

"Shh," Brannon cautioned with a whisper. "It doesn't make sense. If they got that angry at the school, obviously they would barge over here and cause trouble!"

"But I can't see anyone. Can you?" she pressed.

Brannon bent over to whisper. "No, but that doesn't mean they're not here."

"Inside?"

"Maybe."

"What do we do now?"

"Knock on the door."

"You're joking."

"If Rutherford and gang are inside with the Fettersons, time is critical. I don't know if they're expecting us or not. Is there a back door?"

"One on the north side, I believe," she replied.

"Go around there and stay back in the shadows. If they come busting out that door, fire that Greener over their heads. That will give them second thoughts about trying to escape."

"If Rutherford steps out that door, I'll shoot a lot lower than over his head."

"Be careful. I hear schoolteachers are tough to replace," Brannon cautioned.

"Mr. Brannon." She paused and cocked her head sideways. "You be careful . . . because I didn't believe all that *bois de vache* about having nothing to lose."

He gave her a few moments to position herself;

134

then he crept up to the front door of the Mercantile. Standing to one side of the doorway, Brannon reached over and rapped on the outside door with the butt of his Winchester.

"Mrs. Fetterson!" he called. There was no answer.

"Mrs. Fetterson?" He thought he heard a faint voice reply, "Who is it?"

"It's me, Brannon. Stuart Brannon." He stepped back away from the door quickly.

At the first splintered blast of a bullet shattering the outer door, he rolled to the dirt and positioned himself to fire on any man blazing his way out.

He tried counting shots but lost track at about eight. Each one ripped through the wooden outer door of the Mercantile. Brannon could see that the door was actually shot in half. Two pieces swung helplessly from the hinges.

First Brannon thought he could make out the barrel of a revolver, then an arm, and a shoulder. Then a man cautiously stepped to the doorway, pointing his gun into the darkness.

Brannon hesitated.

Would they push Fetterson out the door first?
He waited.

Finally, the man called back to those inside. "Cleve, I cain't see nothin' out here!"

"Drop the gun, Mister," Brannon called out through the dark.

Instead the man spun and fired off several shots at Brannon. All the shots were high.

Brannon's weren't.

135

The bullet from the Winchester caught the man in the left shoulder, spun him around, and he collapsed back inside the store with only his feet sticking out on the wooden sidewalk. Soon he was pulled back inside.

Suddenly, a blast sounded from the north side of the building, followed by an explosion of yells and curses.

She was on her own and Brannon knew it. He couldn't leave the front door uncovered. She wouldn't want him to.

"Brannon!" a voice screamed out the open front door. There was no response.

"Brannon! I know you're out there. Listen to me! Brannon?" the voice yelled.

Brannon rolled over to a closer position and waited.

"Brannon! Call off your men, or you may never see Mrs. Fetterson alive!"

He thought he could see one of the shuttered windows in front of the store barely start to open.

Is that a gun barrel? Does he think I'll show my position?

Brannon yanked off his hat and spun it through the night shadows towards the front of the store. Three rapid reports and flashes of gunfire blazed from the window.

Using his Colt, Brannon squeezed off one round, which was followed by a scream as the pistol dropped to the sidewalk and the hand disappeared back inside the building.

Within moments another thunderous discharge

came from the north side of the building. Boards rattled this time.

"She lowered her sights," he mumbled to himself.

At the blast he dove for the open doorway.

If they're all at the back door, I'll have a chance. I can't stop at the doorway because the night light will silhouette me. Even one of those old boys couldn't miss a target like that.

Brannon rolled across the floor and crouched behind what he remembered to be barrels of nails. With Winchester on the floor next to him and Colt in his hand, he waited for the others to make the first move. He heard voices and footsteps shuffle back into the front storeroom.

"He's got a dozen men out there!"

"Where's this Brannon going to get a dozen men!"

"We know there's two or three guns out front."

"I say he's just got the Irishman and maybe one other. In another hour it's daylight. We've got position and supplies. We'll just sit tight."

"Sit tight? I'm bleeding to death!"

"You go out that door, Brannon will shoot you down. He's a killer."

"Maybe we can talk our way out of here."

"We're goin' to keep them doors covered and stay right here."

"I'm with you, Lindsay. I've had enough."

"I've really got to find a doc. Cleve, you and Thrush can stay here and do Rutherford's dirty work."

"You boys ain't leavin'! Nobody leaves Dixon Rutherford."

"What do you mean, nobody?"

"Now you boys don't think that Irishman shot Loredo, do ya?"

"Ya mean, Dixon shot him . . . when he was tryin' to quit?"

"I'll be —"

"Well, maybe so, but Dixon ain't here!"

"He don't forget. You'll never even know he's around. Jist a bullet in the back of the head."

"Boys, Cleve may be right —"

Suddenly Brannon heard men scuffling and a punch or two thrown. His eyes adjusted slightly, but he still couldn't tell who was fighting whom.

"I got his gun!"

"You boys will regret this every day of your short lives!"

"Thrush . . . you declare yourself right now. I ain't waiting for an answer."

"I been shot at, pistol-whipped, and jist about took a shotgun blast in the side of the head. That's enough for me too. I'm ready to *pasear* right out of here."

"Brannon!" a man shouted. "My name's Lindsay. Look, I've got Cleve at gun point. Rutherford's not here; neither is Mrs. Fetterson. That was jist a bluff. Call off your men. We want a little palaver."

There was silence.

"Brannon!" he screamed. "What do you say, Brannon? We ain't gunmen on the peck!"

"Drop the guns and face the door!" he shouted.

"What the —"

"He's in here!"

"We're dead!"

"Drop 'em all!" he barked. The guns crashed to the floor.

"Cleve, I've got this Winchester pointed at you first. Anyone makes a sudden move, and I'll gut-shoot you. I don't intend on you runnin' off again. Whichever one of you is Lindsay, I'd appreciate it if you'd light a lantern. If you make a break in this dark room, I don't know how many I'd have to shoot in order to hit the right fella."

A match flashed at a man's side and flickered toward a counter. Then the dull glow of a paraffin lamp reflected hardened faces.

"Let's get this thing clear from the beginning," Brannon began. "I've lost patience with all of you. I don't plan on talkin' much. You go for a gun, and I'll kill you. You make a run for the door, I'll kill ya. Try to go out the back, and that Greener will blow a hole in you the size of a watermelon."

The one named Lindsay spoke up. "Brannon, if you were in here, then you heard what we said. Most of us have had it. We just want to light a shuck. We got no claim in this. We're just workin' for wages."

"That sounds mighty sweet, boys, but you all don't inspire a tremendous amount of confidence." Brannon noticed that Creek had walked silently through the back door and stood behind the men, holding the shotgun on them from the back side.

"Brannon, I need a doc . . . you nearly shot my arm off!"

"Look, Brannon, you heard Cleve admit that it was Rutherford who gunned down Loredo. We surely don't aim to work for no man like that!" Lindsay explained.

"Get some of that cloth over there and bandage up these boys. You've got to stop that bleeding!"

Lindsay turned toward the counter and faced Rose Creek.

"What the —"

Cleve spun his head. "The breed? She had the shotgun? We should have —"

Before he could finish, Creek rushed Cleve and jammed the barrel of the shotgun into his belly so violently that he staggered back, groping towards his now empty holster, then fell across some flour sacks and sprawled on his back on the floor. Instantly, she was on him, with both barrels jammed against his Adam's apple.

"Brannon," he choked, "call her off!"

"I don't tell her what to do."

"You others might not want to watch this," she sneered. "When I pull these triggers, his head is going to separate from his body. It's an ugly sight!"

Everyone in the room watched as she slowly pulled both triggers.

All of them, except Cleve, heard the click-click of two empty chambers.

"They was empty!"

"He fainted!" one of them called. "He done passed out!"

"Stay where you are! Miss Creek can really get mean if you make her mad," Brannon cautioned. "Rose, gather those revolvers on the floor. Lindsay, go ahead and bandage up those boys."

Creek came over by Brannon, and they guarded the four men while two of them were being wrapped.

"What was this charade with Cleve?" Brannon whispered.

"It was sort of a patented Brannon response, wasn't it?" she admitted.

"Well, it wasn't your normal schoolteacher slap on the wrist," he commented. "What provoked all of that?"

"This!" She walked over to the unconscious man and pulled an object out of his belt.

"Your buckskin dress?"

"Yes. He treated it like a trinket. It was my mother's. My grandmother beaded it. No man touches that dress."

"No man . . . ever?"

"Not unless I give him permission. I did not give that dirty man permission."

"Hold this Winchester while I hogtie old Cleve." Brannon grabbed a rope hanging from an overhead beam and quickly had the downed man secure.

"I still can't believe you came in here single-handed and buffaloed all these men," she added when he returned to where she was standing.

"Well, the Lord looks kindly on fools. He gave me a break when I dove through that doorway."

"Nobody gave you anything. It was the steelhard, irrational courage of Stuart Brannon. It doesn't seem like you ever need much help, human or divine."

He stared at her for a moment.

Brannon wanted to protest her statement, but something inside him restrained him.

That's just not right . . . or is it?

Then he turned to the others.

"Listen carefully because I won't repeat this. Lindsay, you take a jar of that liniment to treat those wounds. Grab a string of the dried apples and a package of jerky. I want you out of town. You're going to have to leave the guns here. You ride night and day till you get to Tres Casas and then take these two boys to Doc Shepherd. Tell him that Brannon shot ya, and Brannon will pay the bill."

"That Colt cost me forty dollars!" one man complained.

Brannon looked at the man.

Dirty, scared, hungry . . .

Taking a deep breath and rubbing the back of his hand across his mouth, Brannon sighed. "Look, empty those belts. Miss Rose, you spin the cartridges out of the chambers, and they can take the guns with them."

"You are going to let them have the guns?" she protested.

142

"Yeah, well, I know what it's like to push cattle day and night for three months and have nothing to show for it but stiff joints and a new 'peace-maker.' Take the guns, boys."

Lindsay grabbed the supplies. "Kin we nab a pouch of tobacco? Some of us would like to fill a blanket!"

"Where did they take the Fettersons?"

"We don't know, Brannon, honest! Dixon nabbed Fetterson down at Highsmiths'. Told us to grab the missus and hold the store. He said you'd come back here first. Besides, he mentioned appropriating the building for a new headquarters."

"And Mrs. Fetterson?"

"No one was home when we got here. Dixon and Cleve were a jabberin' down at Highsmiths', so maybe Cleve knows somethin'."

"All right, take the tobacco and some stick candy. Don't look back, don't come back, don't slow down until you get to New Mexico," Brannon warned.

"You fought us, shot us, and treated us square, Mister," one man said. "That's more than Rutherford ever did."

"Look, I gave you a break. The Lord knows we all deserve one. But I won't give you another — ever. Boys, choose your side more carefully next time. This is wild country out here, and there's no room for error. If you're going to get into scrapes, make sure they're worth gettin' shot up for. Don't go off half-cocked fightin' another

143

man's battle. Whatever the wages Rutherford's giving you aren't enough to die for."

"Ya kin say that 'gin. Let's ride, boys!"

The four men slunk out into the night.

"That's the stupidest speech I ever heard!" Creek blurted out. "Don't fight another's battles? Brannon, you've spent the past twenty-four hours fighting other people's battles! I've got a feeling that's all you've ever done your whole life! What you really meant to say was, 'Don't fight Stuart Brannon!' Now if you're through with your moralizing monologue, where are some more shells? My shoulder is going to be black and blue, but I won't carry an empty gun."

He gave her a good lookover before he grinned.

She's just like Lisa. Won't let me get away with anything.

"It was kind of a dumb sermon, wasn't it?"

"Letting them go was dumb. *'Qui fugiebat rursus proeliabitur,'*" she added, glancing to see what reaction Brannon would have to her Latin.

"Tertullian may be right; they might come back to fight another day. But the choice was either that or shooting them. Grab some of those shells in the case. Remind me to pay Fettersons back for these supplies."

Creek paused and looked Brannon in the eyes. "I'm glad you didn't kill them. What about him?" She pointed to Cleve who struggled to loosen the ropes.

"Well, Miss Rose, I don't figure on leaving Paradise Meadow again without the matter of

144

Rutherford settled. Maybe old Cleve here will tell us where he is."

"I ain't telling you nothin'! What did you do with Lindsay and the others?"

"Oh, they wanted to stay and visit, but they had a train to catch."

"Train? There ain't no tracks between here and Denver!"

"Precisely!" Brannon nodded. "Now, where's Rutherford?"

"He's somewhere in the dark with a gun to your back, Brannon. That's right . . . he'll find you, and you'll never even get a chance to whip out that .44!"

"Well, sorry you don't want to cooperate. Rose, let's just march old Cleve here over to the Gold Palace. Can you imagine how furious Rutherford will be that Cleve couldn't hold the Mercantile or the boys?"

He jerked the bound gunman to his feet, gagged him with his bandana, and shoved him towards the front door.

"Rose, if Cleve here tries to run away from us, shoot his legs off."

She grimaced at Brannon but loaded the shotgun. Slinging her buckskin dress over her shoulder, she closed what was left of the front door and joined Brannon. He walked El Viento behind Creek and the bound Cleve.

The fire at the jail was down to a dull glow, but sparks still whipped into the air. As they headed in that direction, Cleve stopped and turned

145

to Brannon as if wanting to speak. Brannon shoved down the gag.

"Brannon, I'm a dead man if you march me into the Gold Palace. Rutherford doesn't look lightly on failure."

"Is that where he is?"

Cleve nodded.

"And the Fettersons?"

"He drug off Fetterson, but I don't know about the wife. Honest!"

"Why Fetterson?"

"Because he stood up against him. He can't let something like that happen. Brannon, Dixon goes plumb wild when he don't get his way!"

"What's he going to do with him?"

"What do you think?" Cleve challenged him.

"He can't kill an innocent man!" Creek gasped. "Not even in this town."

"Look," Cleve pleaded, "I told you all I know. Now don't shove me into the Gold Palace with my hands tied."

"Will you be willing to tell all of this to a judge? Including the part about Loredo?"

"What judge? There ain't no judge in Paradise Meadow except Rutherford."

"Well, now that's the difference between you and me," Brannon replied. "I figure we'll be judged for just about everything we do. Now if I send down to the county courthouse and have them send up a judge, will you tell your story?"

"Rutherford would kill me if I did that."

"Then just remember, it was your choice. Come on."

"Wait! I'll do it. I'll talk to a judge."

"Rose, can you make it on your own over to where young Gilmore is camped?"

"I suppose. Why?"

"Take Cleve with you. Hold him until I show up. I don't think anyone will be looking across there."

"What if Hawthorne Miller won't allow such a thing?"

"Tell him I'll pay him for any inconvenience. Men like that will do anything for money."

"And you? Will you go into the Gold Palace alone?"

"Only if I have to."

"Brannon," she said hesitating. "Brannon, your luck is going to run out. You know that, don't you? You're not invincible."

"Yeah," he agreed. "Then it will be up to providence."

"One day —" She stopped and then turned back to Brannon. "One day your providence will run out too."

She shoved the shotgun at Cleve, and the two of them disappeared into the night.

Brannon figured it would be less than an hour before break of day. His movement was concealed in the dark, but so was Rutherford's. He led El Viento towards the Gold Palace.

How many more men does he have in Paradise Meadow?

Did Lindsay and the others really ride out of town?

Where's Mrs. Fetterson?

Lord, this thing is getting worse and worse!

Why in the world didn't I just ride off to Arizona and mail Mulroney the money?

The mild western wind had not slacked, yet Brannon felt chilled. His fingers were cold. His pace was stiff. And for the first time all night, he was tired and sleepy.

He had spent most of the past twenty-four hours in armed confrontation. Little seemed to have improved.

In the shadows of the night every man could be an enemy.

Or every man a friend.

He envied Lindsay and the others.

They just rode away. No guilt. I can't do it, Lord. I never know how to quit. Lisa was right. I can't do anything halfway. I can't force myself to leave. And I'm having a tough time pushing myself into another fight.

Why did Rose say that? Why did she say my luck would run out? Providence run out? What does that mean? And that line — what was it? . . . 'I will not cry seven days for you if you die.' I don't know why she said that! I have faced harder cases than Dixon Rutherford. And crazier ones too.

"Mr. Brannon!" a voice sliced through the now graying skies.

He spun with both hands on the Winchester.

"You need some help!" the voice called softly.

"What? Who are . . . Highsmith? You're Mr. Highsmith." Several men approached the street from behind a large cookhouse tent.

"Yes, sir. And these are a few of the others around town who think it's time to challenge Mayor Rutherford."

"He ain't no mayor," one man called. "Nobody ever voted for him."

"Where's Fetterson?" Brannon asked.

"Don't know. Dixon showed up to question him. The next thing I knew, a bunch of his boys started hurrahing the schoolhouse and knockin' down our place. I grabbed my wife and pulled her to safety, but by then Henry and Rutherford had disappeared."

"And Mrs. Fetterson?"

"She was on her way to our house, so I took the ladies over to the Gleackners'. I scouted up these men and started towards the jail. Then we spotted you. Mr. Brannon, we ain't professional shootists, like yourself, but Paradise Meadow is sick and tired of Rutherford. We're ready to make a stand."

"Look, eh . . ." Brannon stammered. "You men, well, this isn't a game. Bullets are going to fly, and somebody is liable to catch a few."

"Mr. Brannon." A man in the back stepped forward. "Henry Fetterson stood right there and took a beating for every decent person in Paradise Meadow. We've got to do something for Henry."

"We'd be ashamed to live with ourselves if we don't try to help."

"Brannon, you just drifted in and we don't know you. But a man can't live in fear every day. We've got to wake up in the mornin' and look our neighbors in the face. Now I don't know if that makes sense to you at all . . ."

Brannon glanced at the determined faces waiting for his leadership.

Paradise Meadow? Maybe this could be a paradise for some after all!

"Which place is the Gold Palace?"

"The one with the horses hitched out front, next to Leroy's."

Brannon gazed at the tent-topped building.

"How many doors does it have?"

"I guess one in the back and one on the street," Highsmith reported.

"Do they sell food in there?"

"Yeah, sure. They never close."

Brannon motioned the men to step closer. "Go in there without the rifles and order up some breakfast. Keep your handguns holstered." He began to single them out. "You two go in together, just like you were starting a new day. Then in a minute this man will enter. Go over and sit by your friends. Make sure all three of you are right by that canvas wall on the south side."

Pointing to a short man with a drooping mustache, he said, "Friend, we'll need you to hold the rifles out on that south side. As soon as I draw my gun, one of these men will slice a hole in the canvas, and then you hand those rifles inside. Highsmith, you guard the back door."

150

Turning back to the short man, Brannon instructed, "When you've finished, whip around to the front and guard that door. We'll try to rescue Mr. Fetterson and capture Rutherford."

"How will we know what to do?" one of the men asked.

"I'll come in after you are settled and make a play. You'll know. Are you ready?"

They nodded.

The first two men walked off into the early morning darkness toward the Gold Palace.

Highsmith went to the back entrance, and the short man, staggering with an arm load of rifles, camped at the side of the building.

The last man entered the Gold Palace. Brannon watched as a couple of customers staggered out and gazed at the stars.

One man slurred, "Pinky . . . it ain't even daylight!"

They turned around and stumbled back towards the entrance of the Gold Palace.

Brannon spun the chamber of his pistol and filled the sixth hole. Then he shoved several bullets into the breech of the Winchester.

Three men walked their horses toward the saloon and tied them out front. Brannon tied El Viento alongside them. As they started to enter, he slipped up behind them, pulled his hat low, and followed them through the door.

EIGHT

The Gold Palace.
Every western settlement of more than a dozen folks had one like it.
Some people labeled them "dens of iniquity."
Others found in them a dark, smoky place to hide.
Still others saw them merely as a convenient place to cut the road dust and grab a greasy meal.
And for a few — they were home.
They could be made of adobe, wood, canvas, brush — or a combination of these. They all had a long bar, an assortment of rickety chairs and tables, a faro spread, a brass spittoon, just barely nonlethal whiskey, and a bartender that never held a job longer than three months.
Fortunes were occasionally won, lost, drowned, or given away. But most of the time huge strikes of gold remained safe, tucked away in the dreams of the patrons. Every man wore boots and at least one sidearm, and no one ever asked another to remove his hat.
Brannon had never set foot inside the Gold Palace before, but he knew exactly what he would find. The three men ahead of him walked straight to the bar. He trailed them for about six steps, which gave his eyes time to adjust. He spotted

Rutherford sitting at the back of the building. The mayor was forking down breakfast and debating with another man at the table.

Well, he's got to have at least four or five men in here — but which ones? He's too vain to shoot me down without making a grandstand play.

Rutherford hardly looked up as Brannon approached the table.

He thinks I'm walking into his trap . . . maybe I am!

Rutherford pushed his tin plate back and picked his teeth with his knife.

"Brannon, you're under arrest for killing Frank Hughes at the edge of town this morning, for breaking the Irishman and the twins out of jail, for criminal assault upon five Paradise Meadow citizens including the town marshal, and for the slaughter of my brothers Harlan and Oake over a year ago!"

"Rutherford, I want to know the whereabouts of Henry Fetterson!" Brannon rested his hand on the grip of his pistol.

The mayor glanced at the man sitting next to him and flashed a sinister smile. Then the expression slid into a scowl as he glanced back up at Brannon.

"Maybe you didn't understand. You're under arrest for murder!"

"Let's get one thing straight, Rutherford. Without these boys sitting around the room, you wouldn't have the nerve or the talent to arrest a flea for riding on the back of a dog. Frank

Hughes was killed because he was trying to collect your blood money. He attempted to bushwhack me on two different occasions. He failed. I want to know where Fetterson is, and I want to know right now!"

"Brannon, let me make myself clear. You can be carried out of here feet first. Or you can wait until we try you and hang you. My own preference would be for you to make some foolhardy play right now. It would be a lot quicker. On the other hand, having the famous Stuart Brannon swing from our hanging tree does have a certain attraction."

"You know, Rutherford, your brothers were heartless, vicious murderers — but at least they had the guts to face us straight on, while you hid back in the woods. Somehow you lived through it, so now you can bully and extort folks too preoccupied with survival to give you much resistance. Well, the party's over. The only one standing trial for murder will be you."

Suddenly Brannon slammed his knee under the table, pushing the entire contents into Rutherford's lap. He scrambled backwards, tripped over his chair, and fell to the floor. He struggled to his hands and knees cursing.

"Brannon, you'd be a dead man by now except for the joy of seeing you hang!"

The mayor stood to his feet. "I've got men all over this room! You pull that Colt and you'll look like a jelly sieve. Maybe you don't know my boys. Boise is holding that scattergun. Logan has the long-barreled peacemaker. Tempest is a little trigger happy, so he holds two revolvers. And Barnes, here, well, Barnes goes wild in a fight and is liable to shoot you, stab you, and bite you all at once. Now, get your hand off that Colt!" Rutherford demanded.

Four and Rutherford? That's all he has left? That means at least a dozen in the room are uncommitted.

He nodded slightly to Highsmith's friend. Most heads were turned towards Brannon, and none saw the rifles being slipped through the canvas wall.

"Thanks for the introductions, but I do know several of your former employees." Brannon's mind raced ahead of his words. "Lindsay, Thrush, and two others rode out of town about thirty minutes ago. Cleve is hogtied and begging to tell a judge all about the sins of Mayor Rutherford."

"You don't expect me to believe —" Rutherford began to huff.

"Oh, I don't give a buffalo chip what you believe. But I'd like these boys to know that it was you who shot Loredo in the back and tried to pin it on Peter Mulroney."

"He did what?" Boise called out.

"He's lying, boys. He's just scared of being lynched and trying to cheat fate."

"I presume you're Boise," Brannon called out. "Well, don't move that scattergun. There seems to be a .50 caliber rifle pointed at your midsection from over on that far side. Saw an old boy down in Tombstone take a .50 from that distance, and

155

they had to put up new wallpaper just to give him a proper burial."

Boise and the others suddenly noticed the three men who were standing holding weapons.

"Those shopkeepers aren't going to pull those triggers!" Rutherford shouted.

"Well, we're all going to find that out soon enough. Now the rest of you men in here, slip out those doors as fast as you can, but keep your hands way above your belts. You see, we've got the doors covered, and it's too dark to see clearly."

"He's lying," Rutherford shouted.

Most in the Gold Palace, including the bartenders and the cook, fled for the doors with hands raised.

"Looks like a standoff, Brannon!" Boise called.

"Nope. We've got the edge."

"How do you figure that?"

"Well now, we've got the doors covered, and these men have already decided that bringing law and order to Paradise Meadow is worth risking their lives for. You men are still trying to decide if Dixon Rutherford is worth laying your life on the line for. That sort of gives us a marked advantage, doesn't it?"

"Did you say Lindsay and the others pulled out?"

"All but Cleve!"

"That's it for me!" Boise drawled. "I never did like this setup, and it sure ain't worth carrying lead for." He tossed the shotgun to the floor and turned towards the front door.

Then everything went crazy.

Seeming to forget the roomful of poised weapons, Rutherford pulled a vest gun from his coat pocket and fired at Boise. The bullet splintered the door facing, and Boise dove into the street. Highsmith's short friend, posted outside, fired at the fleeing gunman. His bullet missed Boise and sailed into the saloon, shattering six bottles and embedding itself into the mahogany bar.

Those inside hardly noticed. Brannon was diving for Rutherford's table. One of Rutherford's men fired two quick shots at Brannon. Both shots went wild, and one of Highsmith's friends instantly shot the man in the chest.

One of the errant bullets ricocheted off the wood stove and slammed into Barnes's leg. Dropping his gun and clutching his wounded leg, he pulled a big knife and lunged awkwardly at Brannon.

But Brannon was on the move. His fist caught Rutherford blind-sided behind the right ear, slumping the mayor to the floor. At that moment Brannon felt Barnes's knife cut across his left arm between his elbow and his shoulder.

Brannon grabbed his wounded arm and stumbled over Rutherford. Barnes lunged again, but this time he faced Brannon's survival instinct. Abandoning his wounded arm, he pulled his second gun from his belt and fired two shots. The impact of the bullets slung Barnes across the room.

The fourth man hesitated as bullets flew, and one of the shopkeepers nervously fired in his direction. The bullet ripped through the canvas upper wall, and the gunman dove out through the hole into the alley.

Brannon heard more shots outside as one of the shopkeepers ran to his side. He sat up to examine his wound.

"Mr. Brannon, where'd you get shot?"

"I took a blade in the arm. Tie it up for me!" he called.

Suddenly everything started to fade, and the voices sounded distant. Then he could hear no voices at all.

Rose Creek was still talking to a sleepy Hawthorne Miller when she heard the first gunfire from the Gold Palace.

"Look, all I'm asking is that you keep a gun on this man until the matter is settled." Her head spun with the second blast.

"Jeremiah," she pressed, "will you hold a gun on this man?"

"Miss Rose, I . . . eh . . ." He glanced at Miller. "Yes, ma'am, I will!"

She shoved the shotgun into Gilmore's hands.

"We'll keep him here under one condition," Miller puffed.

"Oh?" Creek looked over at the photographer.

"A sitting with you in your buckskins and Brannon at your side," he demanded.

"Here, Jeremy can hold the buckskin." She handed the dress to Gilmore and turned to leave. Several more shots rang out.

"I get the picture?" Miller shouted.

"If Brannon's alive!" she called back. Lifting her long dress above her ankles, she ran across the footbridge and circled the still smoking remnants of the jail. Dawn finally broke in the east, and the winds still blew from the west.

If he's alive? Brannon, you'd better be alive!

She reached the Gold Palace in time to see Mr. Highsmith standing over a slain gunman. A short man with a big mustache held a gun on another of Rutherford's men.

"Where's Brannon?"

"Inside."

"What happened? What are you doing here?" she stammered.

"We joined up to help Brannon, but I don't know what happened in there. From the sounds of it he's been hit."

Creek grabbed the slain gunman's pistol and hurried toward the front of the saloon. A crowd of men stood about twenty feet from the door out in the street.

"Don't go in there, Miss Rose," one man cautioned. "Bullets is flyin' ever'where!"

She didn't hesitate. As she barged through the door, the bystanders scurried up behind her to look from the safety of the wooden sidewalk.

Several armed men stood around Rutherford. He was down, but seemed to stir. She could see two other men sprawled across the floor and one man bent over Brannon.

"Is he dead?" she called as she ran to his side.

"Miss Rose!" the man started. "What . . ."

She straddled Brannon and lifted up his head. There was a pool of blood on the floor by his left arm.

"Brannon! . . . don't you go dying on me! You hear me?" she cried. "I've got plans, Brannon, and they don't include you dying!"

Her vision began to blur, and she could barely hear herself rant, "Jimmy, don't go down there! Please, Jimmy!"

The first thing he remembered was that his left arm felt like it was leaning against a hot stove and someone was screaming at him. When his vision cleared enough to distinguish faces, he realized that Rose Creek sat on his stomach shaking his head.

"Rose? Rose!" he mumbled.

"Well . . ." She sniffed wiping her eyes on the sleeve of her dress. "You'd better wake up!"

He could see the tears rolling down her cheeks, but he didn't dare mention it.

"Help me up." He struggled to his feet and clutched her shoulder to keep his balance. "I think I lost a little too much blood too fast."

"Did you get it bandaged?" he asked the man at his other side.

"Pretty fair, Brannon. But a doc ought to tend to that," the man replied.

Highsmith and the short man with the mustache led the captured gunman back into the saloon.

"What about this one, Brannon?" Highsmith motioned to the man. "Shall we just shoot him?"

"What happened to the man who dove out the side?"

"He came blasting out, so I shot him dead."

"Boise, here, was just leaving," Brannon announced. "I believe he was goin' to Texas. Isn't that right?"

"Yes, sir . . . that's exactly it."

"He tried to shoot his way out!" the short man reported.

Brannon walked over by a lantern and examined his bandaged arm. "Bullets came out the front door, all right, but they were from Rutherford's gun," he explained.

"They was? You mean, Dixon was trying to kill him?"

"Yep."

"Well, if Rutherford was trying to shoot him, he cain't be all bad."

"Wasn't his gun still holstered when he dove through that door?" Brannon questioned.

"Yes, sir, I reckon it was."

He looked back at the captured gunman. "Boise, I'd suggest you pull for the Rio Grande in a big hurry. Folks in this town are losin' their tolerance." Brannon motioned to the door.

"You gonna let him go?" Highsmith complained.

"We got more than we can hold right now." Brannon picked up both his Colts, jamming one back into his holster and the other into his belt. His left arm hung limp. "Get on out of here, Boise!"

161

"Yes, sir, I'm gone."

The gunman turned at the door.

"Brannon, I owe you a favor for this one . . . and I don't forget," he called.

"Yeah, well, that old boy out in the trees yesterday morning forgot, and he's dead," Brannon replied.

Boise ducked out the front door.

"Brannon, you don't have any authority to let that man go!" Highsmith cautioned.

"I don't have 'authority' to stop a hanging, a pistol-whipping, or a murdering extortionist either. If you want, I can ride right out of here, and you men can wait for 'authority.' But I'll tell you one thing, we can't shoot everybody who ever worked for Rutherford, and we don't have a jail to hold them."

The tone of his voice caused Highsmith to take several steps backwards.

Brannon continued, "You suppose you could find any handcuffs or shackles over at the jail? Grab me a rope; we can at least tie up Rutherford. These other two you can drag out and bury."

"Stuart, you need to have someone look at that arm," Creek insisted.

"There isn't a doc in town, is there?"

"Not any longer, but Mrs. Highsmith was acting as our school nurse."

"You go fetch her . . . and while you're out there, tell that cook to come back in here and scrape us up some breakfast."

Within moments, the bodies were removed, and

customers wandered back inside the Gold Palace.

Highsmith and the others stood guard in the back of the room while Brannon questioned Rutherford.

"Where's Fetterson?"

"Brannon, you have slaughtered your last innocent man in this place! You'll be hanged for this!"

"Hanged? By whom?"

"Why, by the citizens of Paradise Meadow! When they find out their mayor —"

"Their mayor? Since when did you ever do anything but threaten them? You don't believe your own lies, do you? Where's Fetterson?"

"Where are my men?"

"They're all dead or gone, except for Cleve. And as I said, he's quite ready to tell all about your murders."

"You can't prove anything!"

"Well, we'll just let a jury decide that. Where's Fetterson?"

"What do you mean, a jury?" Highsmith broke in. "We don't have any judge around here."

"I sent word to Denver to send up a U.S. Marshal. When he gets here, he can take Rutherford to jail for the murder of Loredo and Janie Mulroney, just to name a few."

"He killed the Irishwoman?" one of the men croaked.

"You don't really think it was an accident that the mayor's main critic got run down, do you?"

"He kilt a woman? He don't deserve to live!"

one man grumbled. "We don't need a judge to figure that out."

"And we got a nice place that Rutherford fixed up for the occasion," another added.

"How about that, Mr. Mayor? These men are starting to think about a lynchin'. Maybe it's time for me to just ride out of town."

"Brannon! I've got something to say to you in private," Rutherford called.

"You can say it in front of these men," Brannon replied.

"It's to our mutual advantage to talk in private!" Rutherford screamed.

Brannon glanced up at the others holding the guns.

"Mr. Highsmith, why don't you all step back down there and eat yourself a plate of biscuits? If Rutherford tries anything fancy, I expect you to lead him down."

"You can count on that," Highsmith responded.

"Yeah, I figured I could." Brannon nodded.

They positioned themselves at a table where they could watch Brannon and Rutherford.

"Now, what's this important matter?"

"Brannon," Rutherford whispered, "Paradise Meadow don't mean spit to you. You're a gunman . . . like me. Sure, we're on different sides of this, but we understand each other. Now, I've got some color set back — I mean a real good poke. Why don't you just put some shackles on me and lead me out of town telling the people you're going out to meet the U.S. Marshal? We get down the road a piece, and I'll split my poke with you. Then you go your way, I'll go mine. You see?"

"That's the deal? Just how big is the poke?"

"Your share would be . . . $5,000."

"$5,000? You want me to sell out a whole town for —"

"Wait," Rutherford whispered. "Look, you got me and I know it. You can have it all."

"$10,000?"

"Yeah, the whole $10,000!"

"You cheated and extorted these people for $10,000?"

"It was a long winter. What do you say, Brannon?"

"Where's the money?"

"I ain't telling until you've made a deal."

"And I don't make deals until I see some proof."

"You don't expect me to reveal my poke? What would keep you from killing me?"

"What's to keep me from killing you right now?"

"Brannon, you're a —"

"Now don't go saying something you're going to regret!"

Rutherford glanced over at the table full of well-armed townspeople.

"Do you know where Flannigan's is? The long log building at the high end of town?"

"I can find it."

"Well, Flannigan's room six has a black valise under the bed. You'll find the stash in there."

Brannon turned to the men at the table and shouted, "Well, boys, it seems the mayor's been holding back on city funds! In his great sorrow and repentance, he wants to make a small contribution to the city. So let's all walk down to Flannigan's and —"

"Brannon, you —"

Brannon shoved a biscuit into Rutherford's mouth.

"Now, Mayor, there's no reason to add blasphemy to your sins!"

Suddenly a huge man nearly ripped the front door off pushing his way inside the Gold Palace.

"They found him! Fetterson! They found Fetterson!" he hollered.

Brannon jumped to his feet. "Where is he?"

"In the jail!"

"Jail?" Brannon stammered. "But it . . . it burned down."

"Fetterson's dead. The jail burned down with him in it!"

Burned him? Lord, no!

Brannon's hard right cross hammered Rutherford to the wall. He slumped onto a bench, and Brannon grabbed his head by the hair and slammed Rutherford into the bench.

Lord! This town needed good men like Fetterson! It's not right!

"Stuart!" It was Rose Creek yelling and pulling at his arm. "Don't . . . Stuart, you're killing him! Brannon!"

He suddenly noticed the full weight of a woman

166

clutching on to his right arm.

"What are you doing!" she cried.

"He burned the jail around Fetterson!" Brannon yelled.

"Vengeance belongs to the Lord!" she insisted.

He tossed Rutherford to the bench and glared at Creek.

Her words didn't say it.

But her eyes reminded him.

Maybe she was right. Maybe providence just ran out.

Most of the rest of that day was a blur to Brannon. He prevented the others from hanging Rutherford on the spot only by turning them towards the task of giving Fetterson a proper burial. Mrs. Highsmith bandaged up his wounded arm. They retrieved the valise with Rutherford's money. Then they had a big funeral for Henry Fetterson . . . and none at all for the three slain gunmen. Fetterson's store was chosen as the best building to hold Rutherford and Cleve until the U.S. Marshal arrived. Finally Brannon got some sleep.

There are times when a good dream can relax a man. It offers a needed break from the conflicts of the day. The fleeting visions of rolling green hills, or fast horses, or desert sunsets can give a man a chance to wake up refreshed.

Brannon woke up tired.

His left arm ached.

It was almost dark.

From a back storeroom in Fetterson's he

crawled off some feed sacks and groped for his hat. Although there wasn't much grip in it, he did manage to use his left hand. But he couldn't raise it above his shoulder.

The Mercantile had a half-dug block house that Fetterson planned to use to store winter ice. It was quickly converted into a jail cell for Rutherford. Brannon made sure that Cleve was shackled to a post in the back storeroom, separated from his former boss.

Both prisoners asleep, Brannon walked out into the merchandise section of the building. Mr. Highsmith tended business while Mrs. Fetterson spent the day with friends.

"Mr. Highsmith," Brannon began, "how's the widow?"

"As you would figure, she's taking it hard. She wants to pull out tomorrow. Says she's got kin in Virginia City, Nevada."

"Can't say I blame her . . . what about the store?"

"Says she'll sell out, but she wants to take the money with her."

"Well, it shouldn't be so tough to find the money. You interested?"

Highsmith stacked some ready-made britches on the shelf. "I hadn't intended on staying here long. Wanted to move on up to the Little Yellowjacket."

"I'm sure there's lots of money in this town," Brannon said.

"You know, it might be tough to raise the cash

for this place. Most folks here have all their wealth tied up in their outfits."

"What do you think she wants for the business?"

"Don't have any idea. You figurin' to buy it?"

Brannon smiled. "Not if I can help it." Then his smile disappeared. "You know, all afternoon I tried to figure out what could have been done differently. Maybe I shouldn't have stepped into that fight at the schoolhouse."

"They probably would have killed him then and there. We should have hung Rutherford before the funeral."

Ignoring Highsmith's complaint, Brannon continued. "You know, the only cash in this town is Rutherford's cache. Maybe Paradise Meadow should buy the store building with that money."

"Sounds good, but what would a town do with this building?"

"City hall? Or the courthouse? Or a jail or —"

"Or a school?" Rose Creek sailed through the front door.

"Miss Rose! Did you get some rest?" Brannon asked.

"Rest? I salvaged most of the school supplies. Went to the funeral for dear Mr. Fetterson. Had a couple of the carpenters take a look at the school. They said it would be impossible to repair, and I spent the rest of the afternoon surveying every building in town for a possible school site."

"And?"

"And this store has the best location, the best

construction, and the best size!"

"Now, see there, Highsmith? Since Rutherford got that money by extorting most everyone in town, it would be fitting for that money to go into civic projects."

"Sounds good to me!"

Brannon turned to Creek. "But there's just one problem. There's no city government in Paradise Meadow!"

"Have an election," she offered.

"You mean —" Highsmith muttered.

"Yes," she continued, "elect a mayor, city councilmen, marshal, and all of that."

"Yeah! And we can elect our own judge. That way we don't have to wait for the U.S. Marshal in order to hang these two!"

"They do get a trial," Brannon cautioned. "And Cleve will take the chair against Rutherford."

"It doesn't matter," Highsmith responded. "We all know they're guilty. How much time should we have before an election?"

"Eh . . ." Brannon pondered. "I suppose a couple weeks would be right."

"We don't want to hold those murderers that long. I'll go talk to some of the others. I believe we could have the election by tomorrow afternoon."

"Tomorrow?"

"Yep. Listen, Brannon, you watch the store, and I'll see what I can organize." Highsmith banged out the door without another word.

"You look a little worried," Creek observed.

"I think all this town really wants is a hanging."

"Well, if anyone deserves it, it's Rutherford," she commented.

"I won't argue that. But I promised Cleve that if he leveled with me about Rutherford, he'd get treated fairly. Now these men who have been too scared for a year to lift a finger are starting to sound like vigilantes."

"Is that bad?"

"Sometimes. Who controls the vigilantes? There has to be a commitment to justice someplace."

"You mean to mining-camp justice?"

"No, to God's justice. There has to be a right and wrong — an absolute."

"Well, I haven't seen a whole lot of God's justice in my life. Anyway, all of that is too serious. Do you think there's a chance of using this building for the school?"

"Yep."

"You're a mess," she blurted out. "Look at that jacket and shirt! Come on, you need to change."

Brannon sat back and watched her as she picked out a shirt and coat for him.

"I presume you prefer dull, lifeless colors?" she prodded.

"Yeah, it fits my personality." He grinned.

"Well, at least they won't be torn and bloody. Do you want me to rewrap that wound?"

"I think it's all right. Just help me pull off this jacket."

Brannon tugged off his worn shirt in the back

room and pulled on the new one. Then he struggled to slip on the jacket.

"Stuart Brannon, if you shaved, you could look fairly decent," she said laughing.

"On the verge of fairly decent? I'll take that for a compliment. Hand me those things in the pocket of my old jacket."

Creek pulled out some papers, a snub-nosed pencil, a couple of matches, a folding knife, and a gold locket. She opened the locket before handing it to him.

"She's beautiful . . . Stuart Brannon! Are you a married man? Do you have a wife and children? Listen, if you —" Then she caught herself as she saw his wide, easy smile.

He looks years younger when he smiles like that.

Finally, he looked up at Creek. "My Lisa and the baby died in childbirth about two and a half years ago."

She just stared at Brannon. Her mouth fell open. Her eyes began to cloud.

"I . . . I," she stammered, "I didn't know. I . . . I thought everything you ever did, I mean . . . I guess your luck's run out before."

He hardly heard her words. He glanced back at the tiny little picture not much bigger than his thumbnail.

"She is beautiful, isn't she?"

NINE

There are times when the only thing worse than bad government is no government. Paradise Meadow had stumbled along for almost a year under the oppressive self-appointed tenure of Dixon Rutherford. Most folks didn't stay in the area long enough to care whether justice prevailed.

But times change.

Among the current residents of Paradise Meadow some had decided that this was as far as they would go. They had traveled from Kansas and Texas, from California and Nevada, from Europe and the Orient . . . but this was their final destination, and they were determined to make it a decent place to live.

But there were others. Those who hung out along Del Oro Street — prospectors, gamblers, saloon owners, and drifters — who had little use for any government and demanded only a reasonable chance at not getting shot in the back.

These two groups now found only one thing in common — hatred for Dixon Rutherford. The merchants were pushed to barely controllable outrage over Henry Fetterson's and Janie Mulroney's deaths. And it began to dawn on the Del Oro Street rowdies just how much they had been gouged when, upon Rutherford's confinement and the demise of his gunmen, the prices dropped quickly by 25 percent.

As for holding an election — just the talk of it divided the town. Brannon stayed out of the discussion as much as he could and made it his duty to see that the two prisoners were guarded and supervised. Rutherford had grown sullen, refusing to talk to anyone and barely eating his meals. Cleve, on the other hand, grew increasingly frightened by the rumors of lynching. That subject occupied his every conversation.

After a restless night of trying to guard the prisoners and prevent rolling over on his wounded arm, Brannon staggered out of the storeroom to unbolt the front door of Fetterson's store for Emerson Highsmith.

"Mornin'," Brannon greeted him, then meandered to the back of the room looking for a bowl of water. "I didn't attend that meeting last night. What did you decide about the election?"

"The incredible hard-heartedness of those people is appalling!" Highsmith replied.

"The Del Oro Street crowd?" Brannon surmised.

"Yep."

"What happened?"

"Well, we couldn't agree on anything except hanging Rutherford and Cleve."

"After a proper trial . . . right?" Brannon cautioned.

Highsmith stared at him for a minute. "Oh,

yes, yes. But really, Brannon, they refused to support an election today. They said they wanted it to be next Sunday afternoon."

"Sunday afternoon?"

"Yep, and not only that. We suggested that only citizens who had established a permanent residence be allowed to vote, but they insisted that every man in town on that day be given a vote."

"What's at stake here? Obviously they figure that they can pull in the Saturday night crowd and sober them up to vote by Sunday afternoon. But why are they so interested? What's the difference to them?"

"Well, they don't want any laws, taxes, or lawmen interfering with activity along Del Oro Street. And they have their ideas about what to do with that money taken from Rutherford."

"Oh, what's that?"

"Give $50 cash to every person in Paradise Meadow."

"So those old boys who wander in here on Saturday night will get to vote on Sunday and get $50 on Monday . . . which they will probably turn around and spend on Del Oro Street. Sounds almost like buying votes, doesn't it?" Brannon nodded.

"That's exactly what I told them."

"So what did they say?"

"They said if we didn't come around to their way of thinkin' that they might form their own separate town."

"Glad I missed the meeting." Brannon shook his head. "So what was the conclusion?"

"We're having another meeting at two o'clock this afternoon."

"Where?"

"Here."

"In the store? It'll be a bit crowded," Brannon commented.

"Not by 2:00. Mrs. Fetterson is pulling out today."

"Did someone buy this place?"

Highsmith began to box up some of the store supplies. "Nope. But a Dutchman with a couple of freight wagons made it into town last night from the mines up on the Yellowjacket. He sold out everything and was headed to Tres Casas to reload. When he found that Mrs. Fetterson wanted to sell, he agreed to buy all the supplies. She consented to the deal and left me in charge of selling the building. The Dutchman will be over soon to start boxing up."

"Do we need to find a new jail?" Brannon asked.

"Oh, no . . . not yet anyway. She was happy to have you stay here. She didn't sell the furnishings in the back rooms. It's only this merchandise that goes."

Rose Creek stopped by at about ten o'clock. The last of the supplies were being loaded on the freight wagon, and she volunteered to guard the prisoners while Brannon checked on El Viento.

The talk of a quick hanging had all but died out, due to the increased interest in holding elections. Still Brannon worried about leaving her alone to guard the pair. At times he could envision Lindsay, Boise, and the others returning in a flurry of gunfire to try to rescue Rutherford.

The livery on the far side of town near the hanging log had given El Viento excellent care. He was stabled near the street because so many townspeople wanted to look him over. El Viento's regal stature dwarfed the other horses.

Brannon found Leroy at the tent-top cafe and asked him to bring two meals a day over to him and the prisoners. Then Brannon picked up a box of cartridges from a man selling hardware from the back of a wagon.

It was clear . . . mild . . . and dry. The perfect day for riding long distances. And that was exactly what Brannon wished he could do.

Finally, he pushed open the door to Fetterson's and found Rose Creek stepping off the big empty room.

"Lining up school desks, I presume," he observed.

"Oh, yes. It really is just perfect. Living quarters in the rear, and the storeroom could serve for special activities when the weather is too severe to go outside," she mused.

"Sounds like you've closed a deal already." Brannon cautioned, "Highsmith said there was a difference of opinions about what should happen with the confiscated funds. It all depends upon who wins this election."

"Yes, I know all about that. But I don't think this building will deplete the whole account, and I really can't see how anyone would object to money going to provide a school," she offered.

"Well, Miss Rose Creek, contrary to what you might have studied, not all folks care two hoots about schools and education. But I'm not sure both sides can even agree to have an election."

She left him with the empty room, two prisoners, and a slight smile. Brannon scooted a small table from the Fettersons' living quarters in the rear of the building to the big front room that now contained only counters and shelves. He pulled up a chair behind it and left a small hatchet for a gavel. He also discovered a slightly soiled flag which he draped on the wall behind the desk.

Thirty-eight stars . . . I think that's still right. This must be one of the statehood flags.

Stepping back to take a look, he decided that the room now looked fitting for a town meeting.

Lord, the rest is up to them.

He gave the prisoners their dinner, listened to Cleve babble on about how he had tried to stop Rutherford from spooking the freight wagon that ran over Janie Mulroney, and then set up his guard station at the doorway in the back of the front room. And waited. He figured he could guard the prisoners and look in on the meeting at the same time.

Men filtered in, one and two at a time. As Brannon had figured, the Del Oro Street contingent huddled on one side of the room, and the merchants on the other.

After a few minutes, Brannon counted forty-two men and one dog in the room. Highsmith studied his pocket watch, walked to the front, rapped the hatchet on the table, and called the meeting to order. Immediately he was challenged.

"Who gave you the authority to lead this here meeting?" a voice shouted from the Del Oro Street side.

"Well, someone has to preside at the meetin'," Highsmith explained.

"We should elect a presidin' official," the man suggested.

"And just who is to be presidin' while this selection is taking place?" Highsmith boomed.

The room grew quiet as everyone stared at the Del Oro Street man. Finally, he spoke up. "Let Brannon there supervise this election of a presidin' official. He's the only one who ain't standing on one side of the room or the other."

"Yeah, let Brannon!" another shouted.

"That's fine with me," Highsmith added. Then he turned to Brannon. "What about it, Stuart? Could ya help us get this meetin' started?"

He was still leaning against the door casing.

"I'm afraid I'm tied up here guarding the prisoners." He tried to think of another solution. *This is going to be a mighty short meeting!*

Then he pushed his hat back and sighed. "Look, I'll help you elect a presiding officer if you all promise not to move towards that back doorway.

My old sheriff blood gets riled if someone tries to harass the prisoners."

The crowd murmured agreement, and Brannon strolled over behind the desk.

"Now," he began, "the nominations are open for names of men to be elected presiding official. This is for this one meeting only. Are there any nominations?"

"I nominate Emerson Highsmith," one voice shouted from the merchants' side of the room.

"And I nominate Scrappy Flannigan," a man hollered from the noise on the Del Oro Street side of the building.

"Any other nominations?" Brannon called.

The room was reasonably quiet.

"All right, you have two candidates. Mr. Highsmith and Mr. Flannigan. Now I want this man right here," he pointed to a tall thin man next to Highsmith, "to step up by me and the man with the ivory-handled Colt, you come up here too."

"I've appointed these two men to help me count the votes. They can also vote. Now we are ready for the election of presiding official of this meeting. All those in favor of Mr. Highsmith, raise your right hand!"

Every man on the north side of the building raised his hand. As expected, none did on the south side. After consulting with the others, Brannon announced. "Mr. Highsmith has twenty-two votes. Now all in favor of Mr. Flannigan, raise your right hand."

Again there was a consultation. And Brannon reported to the group, "Mr. Flannigan has twenty votes. Mr. Highsmith is elected presiding official at this meeting. Emerson, come on up and take over."

Brannon retired to his chair in the doorway.

Highsmith began, "I believe we have four things we must decide today. First, the date to have our city elections. Second, who is eligible to run for office? Third, who is eligible to vote? And fourth, which officers do we need? Are there any other matters we must decide?"

Sensing a majority, one of the merchants suggested, "We need to decide what to do with Rutherford's poke and what to do with the prisoners!"

Shouts and accusations flew from both sides of the room. Highsmith tried to bang them quiet. Finally, it was Brannon who got their attention.

"Listen, I thought the purpose of the elections was to have a city council that could make those types of decisions."

The Del Oro Street crowd, knowing they would be outvoted anyway, quickly agreed with Brannon.

Highsmith stared at Brannon, then looked back. "He's right. All other matters will be decided after the election! Now I propose elections to be held at this time tomorrow!"

The entire room broke out in heated debate. Brannon listened to the fracas for a few minutes and then went back into the storage room.

At this rate, it will be summer before they agree on anything!

He heard a rap at the side door. He removed the beams that kept it locked, pulled his pistol, and peeked outside. Rose Creek stood there with an unopened parasol in her hand.

"Rose!"

"May I come in? I couldn't stay away any longer. What have they decided? Will we get the building for a school?"

"In their present mood they couldn't decide whether a skunk stinks. So don't hold your breath about the school. Come in and sit a while if you like."

She sat down in Brannon's chair. He sat on the floor with his back to the wall and his Winchester lying nearby.

"How's your arm?"

"Stiff . . . but not burning as bad as yesterday."

"What do you think is going to happen in there?"

He shrugged and pulled the front of his hat down over his eyes. "I have no idea."

"Stuart, what are your plans after this big election?"

"Well, I would hope that a couple deputies from the U.S. Marshal's office show up. I'll turn over the prisoners, make a statement, and ride on down to Arizona."

"What's in Arizona?"

"A deserted ranch house and the bones of hundreds of cows, I expect."

182

"You have a place?"

"Yeah, I hope it's still there."

"You wouldn't think of staying around here?" she questioned.

"Nope. I promised myself no more winters in these mountains. How about you, Rose? What's the future hold?"

She leaned back in the straight wooden chair and spun her closed parasol. She noticed the room was shadowy and dark in a comfortable sort of way. Voices still boomed from the front room.

"If Paradise Meadow elects a mayor and council that wants to put down roots and build a community, then I'll stay and operate the school. If they vote the other way, I guess I'll look for another assignment."

"Do you ever think about going back to the Indian Territory?"

"Only when I'm really depressed."

"Since we sent your only students down to Tres Casas, just who is going to attend school?" he asked.

"Something is in the air. Several different children ran up to me today and said, 'Miss Rose, my daddy says I can come back to school!' But I had to tell them to wait until we have a building."

"Kind of like an answer to prayer, isn't it?"

He glanced up to where she was sitting to catch her reaction. It was a scowl.

"Tell me something, Miss Rose Creek, when did you first get mad at God?"

"What do you mean?"

"You studied the Bible and all about Christ at the seminary, right?"

"Of course, it was required curriculum."

"Well, when did you give up on it?"

"You don't let me slide by, do you, Mr. Brannon? You enjoy challenging me at every step. You remind me of Jimmy."

"Who?"

"Never mind."

"Listen, you don't have to answer," Brannon offered. "But I've got the feeling it's the kind of thing you'd do to me."

"That's probably true. I'm not mad at God . . . well, maybe I am. I don't know . . . for sure. We were given a home that would belong to our family forever. Three times it was burned to the ground. Twice all of our horses were stolen. My father was killed in one of those raids. My brother went down the river one day, and no one has ever seen him since, and my best friend was shot by outlaws just because he had beaten them in a horse race. I prayed that none of that would happen . . . but it did."

"Jimmy?" he asked.

She nodded her head but didn't look at him.

"I wanted to teach in Kansas. I got sent to California. Wanted to teach in Denver. I was sent to Paradise Meadow. I wanted to be known as a good teacher first, and an Indian second. I ended up being labeled a breed. I learned some lessons along the way — lessons from people like you, Stuart Brannon."

"What kind of lesson could I possibly have taught you?"

"That you only get out of life what you can create with your own skill, courage, and bull-headed luck."

"I taught you that?"

"Look, everyone has to find what works for them. You like giving God credit. Well, that's fine, but as far as I can see you've never needed Him for anything. You're able to do whatever you want to do. You just play a little game and call it faith . . . no!" she blurted out.

She jumped to her feet. Even in the shadows Brannon could see her face was flushed. "I should never have said that. That's none of my business, and I had no right to say it! Forgive me, Mr. Brannon. I must be going. Please report to me later what they decided at this meeting."

"Rose! Wait!" Brannon stood to his feet and blocked her exit at the door with his arm.

"Look, it's O.K. to tell me those things. Maybe I needed to hear them. I know how you feel."

"Stuart, you are a white man in a white man's world. You are gifted with courage and marksmanship in a violent part of the country. You couldn't possibly know what I have to live with." She dipped under his arm and scurried down the street.

He bolted the back door once more, checked on the prisoners, and went back to the doorway into the meeting room. He gazed at the heated discussions, but his mind wandered back to Creek's words.

Playing a little game called faith?

It gnawed at Brannon.

It was a double threat.

Of all things, he hated the way people said one thing but meant another. He swore he'd never be that way. His word would be honest, open, true. No hidden motives. No hypocritical actions. No deceitful words.

To have someone insinuate that his actions didn't match his words in, of all areas, the matter of his personal faith distressed him.

There was a second thought that hounded him.

What if she's right?

It was two hours later when the meeting disbanded. Brannon watched the men leave Fetterson's empty store. The last ones, Emerson Highsmith and another merchant, were finishing a discussion as Brannon approached.

"Well, Emerson, fill me in on the highlights. I was in and out and didn't catch everything. I did hear that the elections would be Saturday."

"Yep. That's a slight victory. Actually, it was one of them who suggested a Sunday vote would profane the Sabbath."

"That's mighty considerate in a town that doesn't have a church," Brannon said with a smirk. "Who gets to vote?"

"They got all chunked about that." Highsmith rubbed the palm of his hands together and continued. "We thought we had the votes, so we offered that a man needed to have spent the winter up here in order to vote."

"I thought you had a majority," Brannon added.

"Well, we did, yes, sir, we did. But then three old boys came riding down out of the mines, and I'll be a leppy calf if that Del Oro Street karimption didn't go out and drag them off the street to vote."

"So what is the voting requirement?"

"Any man who's spent three nights in Paradise Meadow in the last month can vote." Highsmith shrugged. "The same is true for holding office."

"Well . . . that's mighty loose. It makes me eligible to vote!" Brannon grinned.

"Yep, it does!" Highsmith nodded. "I suppose that was the selling point."

"What?"

"Well, we got until noon tomorrow to declare the candidates, but the whole room agreed already on who to nominate for town marshal."

"What?"

"Yep. Brannon, you'll be the only candidate on that ballot!"

"But I refuse!"

"They said you'd kick like a bay steer, but it seems you caught us in a bad fix. You happen to be the only one who has both the merchants' trust and the Del Oro Street crowd's fear. So that makes you the man. At least consider it until the U.S. Marshal can make it up here. Look, you're doing the same thing for free now.

187

So you might as well be on the payroll for a while."

"Well, maybe just until the marshal rides into town. I presume you'll be running for mayor?"

"Yeah, I suppose it will be me and Flannigan."

"Mayor, councilmen, and who else?"

"A judge. We want to get them two hung and planted into the ground before someone else gets killed."

"A judge? Who have you got for that unenviable task?"

"No one, yet . . . but we don't need a name until noon tomorrow." Highsmith started to leave the room. "Say — Marshal Stuart Brannon, Paradise Meadow, Colorado. Sounds like one of those dime novels, doesn't it?"

He left Brannon to stand at the doorway and stare at the fading sun.

I could do it. Lord, I'm not going to do it just because I could . . . not any more. Unless You show me different, I'm going back to Arizona.

He turned inside and then caught sight of someone approaching. It was Hawthorne Miller with his wagon.

"Is she here yet, Brannon?" Miller called.

"Who?"

"Miss Rose, of course. The sunlight's just right for that stereoscopic photograph," he boomed.

"What photograph?"

"Why, of you posed next to Miss Rose in her buckskins, of course. Good heavens, she did tell you about the photograph, didn't she?" Miller lurched down off his wagon and hitched the team to the rail. "I sent Gilmore to fetch Miss Rose."

"Miller, I don't pose for photographs. I thought I made that plain to you last fall when you stumbled onto the Little Stephen Mine!"

"Do you mean to tell me that, eh, Miss Rose is not to be taken at her word?" Miller backed away an arm's length from Brannon.

"She promised?"

"As compensation for secreting your infamous prisoner," Miller added pompously.

"Look, I'll pay you for that, Miller, but I don't take kindly to your pressuring Rose —"

"Pressuring? My heavens, Brannon. She volunteered both of your services."

Brannon stepped right at Miller, who jumped back to the protection of the wagon. "Miss Rose did no such thing!"

"Actually, Mr. Brannon, I did."

Brannon spun to see Rose Creek and Jeremiah Gilmore standing on the wooden sidewalk.

"You did what?"

"You told me to tell Mr. Miller it would be worth his while."

"But I meant financially," Brannon protested.

"Oh, I assure you, this will be a successful venture," Miller beamed. "Gilmore, help me with the equipment. We must not waste this sunlight."

"Look, Stuart, I don't like this any more than you. Posing as a trinket in these buckskins for some promoter like Miller is not my idea of dignity. But he did help us when we needed it."

189

Suddenly Brannon realized that Creek had slipped on the beaded buckskin dress and moccasins and had braided her hair.

"Stuart?" she spoke again. "Stuart? What are you staring at?"

"Oh, well . . . I was just thinking, if you go around town like that on Saturday night, you'll have half of Del Oro Street lined up at your front door."

"What?"

"He means, eh . . . you're a handsome woman, Miss Rose," Gilmore blurted out.

"Thank you, Jeremiah. Then you will agree to the photograph? Mr. Miller has promised us both a print for free."

" 'A fronte praecipitium a tergo lupi,' " he countered.

Between a precipice and a wolf? she mused.

Rose Creek smiled at the photographer and jabbed Brannon in the ribs with her elbow.

"So let's make it quick. I don't cherish the idea of standing out here so others can gawk," Brannon added.

The photographs were taken. But not quickly.

For the final pose, Brannon sat on a crate in front of Fetterson's store. His Winchester lay across his lap, his hand was on the trigger, and his hat was tilted back. Miss Rose stood behind his right shoulder. Her braids hung down the front of her buckskin dress, and her hair was carefully parted in the middle. Her hands were folded neatly on Brannon's shoulder.

As per Miller's instruction, neither smiled.

Hawthorne Miller had just disappeared under the black tent that draped his camera when several gunshots ripped through the back of Fetterson's store.

Brannon, Winchester in one hand and Colt in the other, bolted into the building as Miller opened the shutter for the last photograph.

TEN

"Bra — a — a — nnon!" Hawthorne Miller's scream from under the camera tent ricocheted off the storefront windows but somehow missed striking its mark.

At the first shot, Brannon banged his way through the empty Mercantile's front door. Blinded by a half-hour in bright sunlight, he blinked in the darkness. The shots seemed to come from the north side of the building where the back door was braced only by rusty iron hinges and a couple of stout beams. Brannon had no idea whether Rutherford's men had returned to rescue him or if the citizens of Paradise Meadow had come to hang him.

A bullet ripped into the wooden table, and Brannon rolled against the west wall to wait for some target in the doorway.

They're already in the back room with Cleve! I should have known better than to pose for Hawthorne Miller!

"Mister, that bullet was a warnin'! You jist turn around and leave the store. What's happening back here ain't none of your business!" a voice shouted out to Brannon.

"Yeah, there's no reason for you to git all shot up!" another voice echoed.

"You boys are in serious trouble! Now throw down your guns and walk out of there real slow," he called back and then changed positions by rolling over behind the table.

"He thinks he can bluff us out?"

"Mister, you don't know who you're dealing with here. We ain't no bangtails!"

"You're idiots!" he heard Cleve yell. "That's Stuart Brannon in there!"

"Brannon? Sheriff Brannon from Tres Casas?"

"Brannon's in Arizona. I heard Doc Shepherd say so himself!"

"It's Brannon, and you two are as good as dead," Cleve hollered.

"Sheriff Brannon?" a voice called out.

"I'm not a sheriff now, boys. There's no law up here, so there's nothing to keep me from shootin' you on the spot."

"Now look, Brannon, if you ain't the law, then why get all riled up?"

He could hear them changing positions in the storeroom.

"Tell you what, Brannon, you just back out of that room and mosey on over to Slippery Eddie's. We'll finish up our business and come buy you the biggest steak dinner Eddie can fry."

"He don't need no steak dinner!" Cleve hollered. "There's just two of them, Brannon!"

At the sound of a man getting his jaw hammered, Brannon threw a chair through the doorway against the far wall and dove towards the near wall inside the storeroom. As he expected, a shot was fired at the chair.

"Drop it, Chris!" he shouted with the Winchester pointed at the tallest gunman.

"Brannon! It is you!" The gunman almost smiled. "Hey, Leonard, it is Brannon!"

"Howdy, Sheriff," said the other one nodding. Neither dropped his guns.

"Look, either you lay those guns out on the floor, or you'll be laying out on the floor . . . your pick!"

"Brannon, you cain't take us both." Chris grinned. "Can he, Leonard?"

"Try it and one of you is dead for sure and the other one a good maybe. Now put down the guns so nobody gets shot."

"This ain't Tres Casas! Why aren't you in Arizona?" Leonard puzzled.

"It don't seem fair!" Chris echoed.

"Guns down now!" Brannon ordered.

Leonard shrugged and laid down his holster gun. "Sheriff, we was just trying to make a few dollars before we rode on up to Silver City."

While Leonard was giving his apologies, Chris cut behind Cleve, who nursed a sore jaw. Cleve's left foot was shackled to a support beam in the storeroom.

Chris jammed his gun at the back of Cleve's head. "Sheriff Brannon, you give us what we're looking for, or I'll blow this old boy's head off!"

"You're going to shoot Cleve?"

"Is that his name? I thought he was Rutherford. Well, no matter. It ain't nothin' personal, mind ya. But the rumor over at Slippery Eddie's is that this old boy has a poke about the size of a bank vault."

"So you figured to waltz in here and relieve him of his burden?"

"A man can't spend hard money chained to a post," Chris offered. "Besides he done stole the money anyways. Leonard, pick up your gun!"

"Don't touch it, Leonard," Brannon commanded.

"Sheriff Brannon, you jist let me walk out of here with that fat poke, and there don't have to be any more shots fired."

"Chris, I tossed you and Leonard in the hoosegow every other Saturday night for nearly five months. Then on Sunday mornin' I bought you biscuits and gravy and sent you back to the ranch. Now why do you want to go and spoil such a wonderful friendship?"

"It ain't you, Sheriff. Honest, we didn't even know you was up here! We, eh . . . sort of, you know, we was gettin' roostered, so we bragged about grabbing this old boy's satchel, and well, we jist cain't ride away empty-handed. So you give me that poke, or I'll be forced to shoot him."

"Well . . . I guess you got me over a barrel, Chris," Brannon admitted.

"Yes, sir, I do."

"So go ahead and shoot him." Brannon nodded.

"What?"

"Brannon!" Cleve cried.

"I said, go ahead and shoot him. When he slumps to the floor, I'll put a bullet through your skull. I suppose we could bury you both in the same grave. Save on the diggin' that way, wouldn't it, Leonard?"

"Shoot him? Ain't you suppose to be protectin' him?"

"Me? I'm not the marshal. And I can tell you I'm gettin' tired of feeding him and listening to him bellyache. You'll be doing me a favor. Shoot him. Listen, I'll see that you get separate burials. How's that?"

"Now, Sheriff, I wish you'd quit talking about my burial," Chris complained. "Jist tell me where that poke is."

"Well," Brannon drawled, "you understand that this is only because Cleve is such a fine fellow. Rutherford's satchel is right over there on that rafter." Brannon motioned with his rifle.

Still holding his gun at Cleve's neck, the gunman shouted, "Leonard, grab that bag!"

"Leonard!" Brannon dug into his pocket and tossed a coin at the hesitant gunman. "Go buy yourself a good supper at Leroy's and then ride out of town tonight, you hear me?"

"Yes, sir, I'll do that. Sorry, Chris, but I don't think anything in that satchel would be worth going up against Sheriff Brannon."

"Leonard!" Chris shouted, "Leonard Harvey, you git back here!"

Leonard disappeared out the side door, then immediately returned with his hands in the air.

Rose Creek, still dressed in buckskins, held a shotgun to his back.

"Stuart, this one was getting away," she reported.

"Brannon, I jist about got my head blowed off by this squ—"

"Leonard!" Brannon shouted. "There's only one word that will make her pull that trigger, so don't say it!"

"Excuse me . . . eh, ma'am, but I was jist doin' what Sheriff Brannon asked me to," he offered weakly.

"Let him go, Rose. Chris here is the one who's trying to cash in his chips."

"Do you need some help?" she asked.

"Oh, I don't think so . . . do we, Chris?"

Leonard slipped by Miss Rose and into the street.

"Brannon, give me that satchel!" Chris called.

"And you'll ride out of town?"

"I guarantee you'll never see me again."

"Well, that is a tempting offer," Brannon mused. Keeping the Winchester on Chris, he motioned to Creek. "Rose, take that Greener and poke that satchel down off the rafter and hand it to him."

Brannon could see hesitancy in her eyes, but she followed instructions anyway. Chris clutched the satchel and held the gun on Cleve all the time he backed to the side door. Then he sprinted out toward a waiting horse. Cleve heaved a sigh of relief and collapsed to the floor.

Creek lit into Brannon. "You didn't let that saloon sop walk out of here with the town's money, did you?"

Brannon silenced her with his finger to his mouth and mumbled, "Wait." He reached into his pocket and pulled out another coin.

Suddenly, Chris rode his horse right up to the side door and shouted in at them.

"Brannon! This satchel is empty!"

"Of course it is," Brannon hollered. "I can't let you have all that money; it would ruin your character. But you can have the satchel."

"A man can't eat a satchel," Chris complained.

Brannon sidled up to the door and tossed him a coin. "Out of town tonight, Chris!" he insisted.

"Yes, sir . . . and thanks."

He turned to ride off.

"Chris!" Brannon called. "You and Leonard spur on up to Idaho. Straight east of Silver City is the Ace-of-Spades Ranch. You ride up to the big house and tell them Stuart Brannon sent you to look for work. He'll put you on at least 'til winter."

"Thanks, Sheriff. I'm eh . . . you know —"

"Get out of here!" Brannon shouted.

Rose stood by his side as they watched Chris push his horse down the street between the tent houses and stores.

"Brannon, I don't figure you. One minute you're shooting a man and the next buying him supper," she complained.

"Yeah, I've got a definite weakness for good

cowhands. But he didn't do anything more than shoot a couple holes in the hinges and let his liquor do his talking. The main problem is that the back door is ruined. If we don't settle up on these prisoners soon, the whole building will collapse because of bullet holes."

"If the money isn't in the satchel, where is it?" she asked.

"Safe."

"A safe? Fetterson's has a safe?"

"No. I said the money is safe . . . not in a 'safe.' "

"And you won't tell me?"

"Nope. I won't. If you knew, then some lunatic would try whippin' on you to beat the information out. This way, you just don't know."

"That sounds fair . . . I think." She turned back toward the street. "I'm going to change clothes. Do you need some relief on guard duty?"

"Listen, tell Gilmore to go to the old jail and grab one of those iron doors from the timbers and ashes. Have him drag it over here."

"You going to use it as a back door?"

"If I can get it bolted on," Brannon replied. "I presume our photographic session is over."

"Mr. Miller is around in front developing his plates. He was not too pleased with your hasty exit."

Brannon laughed and pushed his black hat back. "No, I don't reckon he was. Well, that's about all he gets out of me."

"I will see that we get our copies." She smiled as she tossed her braids back over her shoulder and left.

Smack dab in the middle between Elizabeth and Lisa, that's what she is! Brannon thought as he watched her walk down the street.

It took until dark, but Gilmore and Brannon mounted the iron bar jail door on the north side entrance, bolting it on all sides.

Brannon stood back to examine their work. "Well, that should slow them down for a while."

"The ones trying to get out, or the ones trying to get in?" Gilmore quizzed.

"Both ways, I hope." Brannon lit a lantern. "Jeremy, how about spelling me a little at guard duty tonight? I'll give you two dollars if you'll take a shift. I'll be out there in that front room asleep. I just need some rest."

"Two dollars, hard money? Yes, sir! Oh . . . let me go tell Mr. Miller," he insisted.

Within ten minutes Jeremiah Gilmore was back at Fetterson's with a Colt peacemaker in one hand and a photograph in the other.

"It's a pretty good likeness, don't you say?" he beamed.

"Well, Miss Rose looks a little startled, and I look as if I'm taking on the whole Apache nation. Is Miller pretty mad at me for cuttin' out on him?"

"Mad? Oh, no! In fact, he says that this photograph will be the center attraction at his exhibition," Gilmore reported.

"What exhibition?"

"Oh, when he returns to New York City. You see, he goes back to New York to publish his books and then introduces them at a photographic exhibition. He says they are quite popular."

"Jeremy, you camp out at that back doorway in the storeroom. If you hear something, just come in and poke me. I'll trade off with you about midnight."

"Mr. Brannon, I heard some men say that you just might be the best gunman in Colorado. Is that right?"

"Gunman? Is that what they call me? I'm just a cattleman."

"Well, some men were talking over at Flannigan's about how you attacked a dozen men down by Conchita. And how you brought in Trevor single-handed, and then you —"

"Whoa! Jeremy don't get too excited. I'm no gunman. Some of those stories are a tad exaggerated. Now I have had to squeeze the trigger a few times, but only if I'm forced."

"Only when you're forced?"

"I don't draw on an unarmed man. I don't point a weapon unless I intend to use it. I won't let a man threaten me, beat on me, or insult me. I try to avoid every fight I can, but once it gets started I intend to win, and to win quick. I don't pay much attention to what people say about me . . . but I pay a whole lot of attention to what the Almighty thinks about me. He'll be the one who does the final judgin'."

Brannon spread his bedroll across the floor.

"Now that might sound like a lot of rules to you when you're young, but a man doesn't live long in this rough and wild country unless he sets some standards and follows them. Well, Jeremiah, that's your lecture for the night. See you about midnight."

It was a deep sleep.
Brannon's first solid rest in a week.
Too tired to roll over.
Too exhausted to snore.
Too worn out to dream.
"Mr. Brannon? Eh . . . Mr. Brannon?"
He didn't want to hear that. He didn't want to hear anything.

Quiet! Stop that chattering! I don't want to wake up. My bones are tired. This bedroll is warm. Go away!

"Mr. Brannon, I'm getting sleepy something fierce."

If I ignore it, it will just fade away!

"Mr. Brannon! It's mornin'!"

He could feel something grab his shoulder.

Look, I said . . .

Suddenly Brannon rolled out of his blanket to his hands and knees and grabbed for his Colt. His hair stuck out sideways. His eyes were bleary. He wore only his long handles. His six-shooter waved in the air. It could have been a comical sight. But at the time, no one was laughing.

"Mr. Brannon, it's me . . . Jeremiah Gilmore!"

Just enough daylight filtered through the front windows of Fetterson's store for Brannon to make out the shadowy figure of a young man standing apprehensively to his left, staring at his drawn gun.

"Jeremy? What time is it?"

"Mornin'."

"Mornin'?" Brannon stood to his feet, rubbed his eyes, pushed back his hair with his hands, and grubbed around for his britches. "Is everything square?"

"Yes, sir. I'm just gettin' tired."

"You been awake all night?"

"Most of it. I think I kind of dozed off a time or two."

"You should have kicked me awake."

"You looked like you could use the sleep."

"You're right about that. Get on out of here and get some rest."

"Yes, sir." He started toward the door. "Mr. Brannon? Listen, if you or Miss Rose need some help, you can count on me."

"Turns your eye a bit, doesn't she?" Brannon teased.

"Yes, sir, she does . . . but I know that you two are stuck on each other. You cut a fine sitting, you do."

Gilmore hurried out the door.

A gunman who cuts a fine sitting with the school-teacher? Sometimes a man needs to see himself from where others stand.

The rest had refreshed Brannon. He and the prisoners ate a big breakfast of bacon, eggs, and beans, and then he walked them out back. The mountain air was still spring-warm and gusty. Once again he thought about riding down to Arizona.

A man could go thirty miles before gettin' hungry on a day like this!

By the time he had both of them locked back up in the makeshift jail, Rose Creek swept through the front door.

"Mr. Brannon, have you heard about the candidates? They have them posted around town. Mr. Highsmith and Mr. Flannigan are running for mayor, plus candidates from both groups for city council. Did you know your name was on the ballot?"

"Town marshal?"

"Yes, you seem to be the only candidate."

"Well, it will be the shortest term in history. The day these men are turned over to the U.S. Marshal, I'm leaving. How about judge? Who's running for judge?"

She raised her eyebrows. "You'll never guess."

"They didn't put me down for judge, too, did they?"

"No. Mr. Hawthorne H. Miller — author, lecturer, photographer, museum director, and former law school student."

"It says all of that on the handbill?"

"Oh, yes, and this is an official ballot. Of course the ink's still wet," she added.

"Well, how does it describe Stuart Brannon?"

"Former Sheriff of Tres Casas, New Mexico

Territory, and noted shootist."

"Who else is running for judge?"

"No one. But Mr. Miller hardly seems like the type to settle into a community to serve as anything, much less a judge."

"You're right about that. I just hope I can leave town before he holds court." He shrugged.

"Stuart, I know you can hardly wait to leave. Well, this is very bold . . . but I would certainly enjoy it if you were to stay in Paradise Meadow for a while. I have enjoyed your friendship in a way . . . in a way that I have not experienced in many years." She looked down at her feet when she spoke. "Actually, it's not what you think," she hastily added.

"What do I think?" he asked.

"Well . . ." She looked up and gazed into his eyes. "I know that no woman alive will ever be able to steal your heart away from your Lisa. It's nothing like that. What I mean . . . I'm saying this rather poorly, aren't I? What I mean is that you have encouraged me, you have been a good friend, and . . . and challenged my faith."

"I challenged your faith?" Brannon asked.

"Those things I said the other day. They weren't really meant for you. I think I was just talking about myself. You have a highly developed sense of right and wrong. I believe it's based on your view of who God is and how He wants you to behave. I envy you sometimes."

"Envy?"

"You seem to understand your strengths and

how they fit into God's design. Me, I'm still wandering around debating whether there's a God who cares at all about a half-breed Cherokee woman. Stuart, you are one of the few people in my life to just accept me for what I am, but when I'm around you, I keep wanting to push myself even further. Anyway, that all sounds like a schoolteacher, doesn't it?"

"Yep."

"Eh . . . is that it? You aren't going to say anything else?" she insisted.

"Nope. But I do plan on doing some ponderin'," he confessed.

"Well, do it quickly because you might just be leaving town sooner than you think," she added.

"Why's that?"

"You might as well read this ballot." She handed him the paper. "The final line says, 'Should Rutherford and Cleve be hung for the deaths of Loredo, Mulroney, and Fetterson?' "

"That's on the ballot? They can't do that! It's a matter to be decided in court. Cleve and Rutherford can't be lumped together!"

"I thought it would get a rise out of you."

"You can't have a public vote on a person's guilt or innocence!"

"Who's going to stop them?"

"I'll go talk to Highsmith. Maybe he can get this thing off the ballot."

"I doubt it." She added, "From what I hear, it was his idea in the first place."

Brannon spent the better part of the day trying to convince the election organizers to remove the referendum concerning Rutherford and Cleve. The whole mention of a hanging seemed to be so popular that no one running for office would even consider abandoning the idea.

About sundown, Jeremiah Gilmore stopped by Fetterson's.

"Mr. Brannon, will you be needin' me on guard tonight?"

"Well, Jeremy, are you feeling up to it?"

"Uh, yes, sir, I am."

"Come on in. I can use the company. What's your boss up to today? Out campaigning, I suppose."

"I reckon so. Mr. Flannigan came over to the wagon this morning and invited Mr. Miller to stop by his place for free drinks, and I haven't seen him since."

"So you had the place to yourself?"

"Yeah, you could say that. It didn't hurt me any to get some rest."

"I bet it didn't!" Brannon laughed. Then he sighed. "I suppose you saw a ballot."

"Yes, sir, you'll be elected town marshal for sure!"

"I meant the part about voting on Rutherford and Cleve."

"Yeah, can they do that? I always thought a man got to have a jury trial."

"Jeremy, laws only work if men agree to follow

them. It seems that folks are set on a hanging."

"What will you do? Will you give them over?"

"I've been asking myself that same question all day." Brannon nodded.

"What did you decide?"

"I haven't."

"Say, did you hear about Garnerville?" Gilmore asked.

"What happened?"

"It's a huge strike. They say you can pick up nuggets as big as cherries right out of the stream. Lots of folks talk about packing up and pulling out."

"Well, that would make a peculiar situation here, wouldn't it?"

"Mr. Brannon, did you ever think about just saddling up and riding away from all of this?"

"About every ten minutes for the past four days."

"What makes you stay?"

"Well, somebody has to look after Miss Rose."

"Sir, eh . . . I would be happy to . . . hey, you're just joshin' me, aren't ya?"

"Jeremiah, did you ever consider being a cow-hand?"

"No, sir, I don't think I ever did."

Brannon and Gilmore talked for a good two hours, and by the time they finished, they had developed a plan. This time, Brannon took the first shift and Gilmore went to sleep. He had no trouble staying awake. He didn't think about Arizona . . . or guarding the prisoners. Instead he kept thinking about Rose Creek's words.

Lord, things are going to spin out of control here, and I don't think I can stop it. I'm going to need a lot more wisdom than I can muster. Don't let me back up. Don't let me get off course!

Around midnight, Gilmore relieved him, and Brannon slept, not expecting any new crisis until after the election.

For once, he was right.

Every man riding into town on Saturday was greeted by two karimptions of citizens, each trying to attract voters to their cause. Some bribed with meals, goods, and drink. Others persuaded by offers of money and the wink of a pretty woman's eye.

Everyone in town was restless and mercurial.

The drifters who expected $50 for their votes knew they'd have to wait until Monday to receive their due. Yet they hankered to light out for the Garnerville diggings. As the day wore on, some began to pull up stakes and move on up the mountain. Others wondered aloud just what kind of town would be left to govern.

The only event they all seemed to look forward to was the hanging. Even that brought some debate. There were those who favored hanging them at 6:01 P.M. Saturday evening. Others insisted they wait until Monday morning.

Most men voted, then hung around the two voting rooms, determined to stick tight until the ballots were counted.

Brannon didn't leave Fetterson's all day.

About 4:00 P.M. when most eyes were focused on the election, Jeremiah Gilmore quietly pulled Hawthorne Miller's photographic wagon around to the north door of the Fetterson's Mercantile.

ELEVEN

Brannon suspected that sometime between sunset and midnight they would come for Rutherford and Cleve.

He didn't know exactly when.

He didn't know who.

The first election ever held in Paradise Meadow concluded at 6:00 P.M., more or less.

Each side scoured town one last time to make sure everyone had voted.

They had.

Some more than once.

The two ballot boxes were packed over to Fetterson's. A crowd soon filled the empty store and overflowed into the street. Grimy prospectors, drifting saddle bums, slickly dressed gamblers, crease-pressed merchants, and semi-sober fortune seekers stood side by side. It was total disorder since no one had been appointed to count the ballots, and each side mistrusted the other.

For a while, Brannon feared the ballots would be destroyed before the counting began. The boxes were shoved and tossed from one man to the next. Two fist fights erupted, but he didn't break them up. Instead, he stood guard at the doorway to the back storage room where the prisoners were held.

Emerson Highsmith tried to calm the crowd. As far as Brannon could tell, no one in the room was listening to him.

"I said . . . would everyone please be quiet! Quiet!" he yelled. Finally, in desperation he pulled his .44 out of his belt and fired into the ceiling. "I said . . ." He was still screaming though the crowd had settled down. "I said for all of you to be quiet!"

"Who put you in charge of this meeting?" someone yelled.

Not again! Lord, how on earth are they ever going to decide anything?

Seizing a brief lull in the roar, Brannon blurted out a suggestion. "Let the schoolteacher count the votes! Everyone knows how reliable teachers are with arithmetic. Both mayoral candidates can appoint one observer, and the rest clear out of the building until the counting is over," he called out.

Highsmith glared at him for a minute. Obviously that wasn't what he had in mind.

"Brannon's right," someone shouted.

"Go get Miss Rose!" another voice added.

"Let's clear out, boys, it's time to do the countin'."

Within a few minutes, Rose Creek parted a sea of men by the front door and entered Fetterson's.

"I hear this was your idea — dragging me into this," she hissed at Brannon.

"I knew you'd be thrilled."

She eased behind the table to open the ballot boxes. As she carefully recorded each vote, the observer for that side waved his hand at the crowd, and a cheer went up.

Vote by vote.

Cheer by cheer.

Brannon tried to keep a tally in his mind, but soon got lost and just waited for Rose to finish and report the results.

The crowd was at a fever pitch when she tallied the last ballot and began her final computations. Then they suddenly hushed.

Creek stood as she announced, "For the office of town marshal, Mr. Stuart Brannon received ninety-two votes, Mr. James Butler Hickok received one vote."

"Wild Bill? Why, he was gunned down holdin' black aces and eights down in Deadwood over two years ago!" a man yelled from the crowd.

"If I'd known that," another wag called out, "I would have voted for him too!"

The crowd broke into a forced laugh that quickly died.

Creek continued, "Mr. Brannon is declared the winner." She turned and nodded at Brannon. "Now, for the office of judge. Mr. Hawthorne H. Miller received twenty-six votes, and someone called 'Ragsy' received twelve write-in votes."

"Ragsy is Flannigan's dog!" one man hollered.

"He don't never do nothin' but sleep behind the bar!"

"Yeah, he's too smart to accept the office," another replied.

"Mr. Miller is declared the winner!"

Rose Creek continued with the results of the races for councilmen. Two members of the Del Oro Street side won seats, as well as two members of the merchants' side.

Brannon had figured earlier that Flannigan would be able to pull in enough prospectors to capture the election for mayor. But with the sudden interest in Garnerville, most of Paradise Meadow's excess population had already drifted up the mountain. The voting could be very close.

It was.

Rose Creek recounted her marks three times before she made the announcement. "For the office of mayor. Mr. Brannon has two write-in votes. Mr. Flannigan has forty-five votes. Mr. Highsmith has forty-six votes. Mr. Highsmith is declared the —"

She didn't finish the sentence.

No one could hear her anyway. Everyone was shouting praise or curses. Brannon, nor anyone else, could tell the difference.

The only thing the crowd seemed united on was that it was time to celebrate. Two swarming masses drifted to respective sides of town, and then, almost as if orchestrated, they rushed back to Fetterson's.

"I wondered how long it would take them to remember the referendum." Brannon took a deep breath and picked up his Winchester.

"Miss Rose?" one of the men shouted. "How about old Rutherford? Do we get to hang him?"

"Yeah, how about it?"

"The vote was fifty-one in favor of the referendum, thirteen against," she reported.

"Do you mean we can hang him now?" another called out.

"I mean," she repeated with obvious contempt, "that the vote was fifty-one in favor of the referendum and thirteen against. That's all I mean!"

"Hey, boys! We get to hang the scoundrels!"

"Somebody grab two ropes!"

The crowd surged toward the door.

"Marshal," one yelled, "it's time for the hangin's!"

"Not yet!" Brannon yelled above the noise. "It's time to go have your election party."

The whole bevy stopped right where they were.

"He's right, boys! I hear Slippery Eddie's is setting up drinks for everyone!"

Within thirty seconds, only Creek and Brannon were left in the building.

"How long before they come back?" she asked.

"Oh, an hour . . . or two . . . or four. But they'll be back before daylight. It all seems easier in the dark. Sort of like God isn't watchin'."

"Are you going to stop them?"

"I'll try. At least I can force them to be responsible for their actions."

"Stuart, why do you do it? Doesn't it seem ironic that you spent half your time in Paradise

Meadow trying to shoot Rutherford and the other half trying to keep him alive?"

"Well, you're the schoolteacher. You can figure it out, I'm sure."

"It obviously doesn't have anything to do with Rutherford, does it?" she prodded.

"Nope. After a fair trial, I believe he deserves to be hung. But this is a matter of law, order, decency, justice, and the fear of the Lord. A town that's ruled by a mob isn't any better than one that's bossed by a man like Rutherford."

"Sounds like a lesson from the French Revolution," she added.

"Well, a town perched up here in these mountains doesn't have a whole lot of chances for survival anyway. But without any respect for the legal system, it will blow itself out of existence."

"That still doesn't explain why Stuart Brannon of Arizona should try to keep this place on the straight and narrow."

"Paradise Meadow is where I happen to be at the time. I don't look for a scrape. But I won't abandon a challenge either."

"Is that the only reason?"

"Nope. I believe that Miss Rose Creek, a cultured and educated maiden of the Cherokee Nation, deserves to have a schoolhouse and a room full of giggling, screaming, crying, yelling children to teach."

"So this is where you make your stand?" She walked over to his side.

"I'll give it a try."

"Well, Mr. Stuart Brannon. This is where I make my stand also. I want that school . . . and I want it to be filled with those children. What can I do to help?"

"I've got things set the way I want them here. But I need an escape route, just in case. I need you to go to the livery and get El Viento. Bring him back here all saddled up. And tote that shotgun of Wishy's as well."

She was back within thirty minutes, and Brannon tied his bedroll and belongings on the back of the horse's cantle.

"I presume your second plan is to leave?" she questioned.

"I want to reserve that option. If a lynch crowd takes over, I'll take it as a sign to get out. You're welcome to join me," he offered.

"Do you really think it will get that bad? I mean, there are still women, children, and families here."

"Frankly, Rose, I believe the town's on the edge of destroying itself. I saw the same thing happen once out in west Texas. This country's too wild, too new, too unsettled. Folks don't know what they want yet. Even otherwise decent folks will do things they never dreamt of back east. They just seem to want to throw off any restrictions they had in the past. So I'll make them choose right here at Fetterson's. This kind of situation seems to bring out the best or the worst in folks. And right now I can't predict which."

She looked at Brannon through the night shadows. "I'm going to teach school. Somewhere, sometime, somehow I'm going to teach."

He stared at her and then smiled. "Yes, Miss Rose, I believe you will. Just hitch El Viento over there by those tents across from the front door."

"Where do you want me and the Greener to park?"

"You stay back in the shadows." Brannon pointed. "Now listen, don't shoot that gun unless to protect yourself. I've got a plan . . . and even though you think it's not working, don't go shooting anyone."

Creek slipped back through the night, and Brannon reentered the store building. He loaded up all the chambers of both Colts, shoved one in his holster and the other into his belt. Then he grabbed up the Winchester, turned the lantern off, and settled in on the floor near the back wall, to the right of the door to the storage room.

They'll expect me to be over there. Well, they're in for more than one surprise!

He could now hear the rumble of a crowd moving across Paradise Meadow. They quickly swarmed to the front of the building, and from the shouts and cheers, Brannon figured most had taken up Slippery Eddie on his offer.

"Marshal, are you in there? We came to get Rutherford and Cleve!"

"Brannon! Open up!"

He cupped his hand around his mouth and shouted back, "Sorry, boys, but we're all closed up! Come back tomorrow."

"Closed? How can you be closed?"

"It's a new law. The jail closes early on election day," Brannon yelled.

"Open up or we'll break her down!"

"Brannon, just turn over those prisoners!"

"Can't do it. I don't have any court order."

"A what?"

"A court order signed by a duly elected judge."

"A judge?"

As the conversation continued, Brannon saw the front door begin to slowly swing open.

They can't really believe I'd let them just walk in.

Silently he rose to his feet. Taking several light steps, he positioned himself behind the door so that just as a man crept in with gun in hand, Brannon laid the steel barrel of the rifle on the man's temple.

"Mister, that cold steel is from a '73 Winchester. Now I suggest you turn around and sneak-pad it right back out of here!"

"Yes, sir! I'll — I'll do that. Yes, sir, I will."

The trembling man back-stepped out the door.

Leaving it partially open, Brannon addressed the crowd.

"I want to see a document signed by the judge ordering me to release the prisoners into your care," he called out.

"We don't need no court order!"

"Well, I do. As marshal I can't legally turn the prisoners over to anyone unless authorized to do so by a judge. You have a judge, don't you?"

"You mean Miller?"

"Yep."

"He's passed out under a table over at Slippery Eddie's," one voice reported.

"Yeah, he won't sign nothin' for two days!"

"I'll wait," Brannon stated.

"Brannon, you ain't officially marshal until you're sworn in!"

"I will turn no man, no matter his guilt or innocence, over to a stewed-up crowd of regulators!"

"If you don't back down, you'll have to face us all!"

"You cain't shoot the bunch of us!" someone else yelled.

"Nope, but I'll hit some of you. Now which of you think hurrying this along is worth dying for?"

"Brannon, they're killers! You're protecting killers. Maybe you cut a deal with those two!"

"We voted to hang 'em, Brannon!"

"I won't turn prisoners over to a lynch mob ever! Now look, boys, I'd do the same if it were you in here."

Brannon could now see out the door into the lantern-reflected faces and noticed Emerson Highsmith and the city councilmen push their way to the front.

"Brannon, we realized that the judge should be in on this, but it happens that he is, as you heard . . . ill-disposed. So the city council in a unanimous decision orders you to release the prisoners to us so that we might carry out the mandate of the voters."

"All the laws I know of for the state of Colorado, County of La Plata, do not give you the authority to interfere with the duties of a duly elected town marshal," Brannon insisted.

A bullet blasted its way into the building, sailed past Brannon, and struck the back wall. He had no idea who fired the shot and did not intend to return fire randomly into the crowd.

"Mayor, you and the city councilmen come inside without weapons, and we'll discuss this!" he called out.

Highsmith came through first, then the others.

"Is there a lantern in here?" Highsmith asked.

"No light . . . too many folks are shot-happy already," Brannon responded.

"Look, Brannon, we appreciate you helping us put the clamps on Rutherford," Highsmith continued, "but to tell you the truth, maybe you've served your time."

"I just got elected," he reminded them.

"But you didn't even want the job!"

"Emerson . . . I expect you to understand this better than the others. If a town lets a lynch mob make the rules, then there are no rules. You and the council will lose control. No one will be safe. You'll find yourselves compromising and playing to the crowd just for your own protection. There are laws higher than this crowd's thirst for vengeance."

"You mean God's?"

"That's right. And you begin to break His laws, soon enough you'll be hating yourself . . . and after that you'll hate each other."

One of the Del Oro Street councilmen spoke up. "I see his angle! It's the money — Rutherford's bankroll! Listen, Mr. Mayor, I make a motion that Marshal Brannon be given $1,000 from the confiscated funds upon his retirement and departure from Paradise and —"

The force of the rifle barrel slamming into his midsection caught the councilman by total surprise and crumpled him to the floor gasping for breath.

"Get him out of here!" Brannon yelled. "Highsmith, the money is right by the door in that Overland sack. Take it with you because I sure don't want it in here! The talkin' is done. I'm delivering these prisoners to the U.S. Marshal. So if you want a fight, send your single men in first because I surely don't want to make any woman a widow!"

The men picked up the money and left the building. Brannon figured it would be several minutes before anyone got up nerve to try anything. He retreated to the back of the room and lifted up several loose flooring boards from what had earlier been the hiding place for the funds. With some effort he slipped down between the floor joists and pulled the boards back over his head.

Grabbing the Winchester with his right hand and one Colt with the other, he crawled face down in the dirt to the far side of the building, waiting for an opportunity to pull himself out from under the Mercantile.

Suddenly someone shouted, "Fire!" He could see the feet of dozens of men run to the north side entrance. At that moment he dragged himself out from under the building, brushed himself off, and ducked into the shadows.

They've set the building on fire! One of the few permanent buildings in this whole town, and they're trying to burn it down. Lord, they're all going insane!

The crowd was so large now at Fetterson's that Brannon had to move slowly around the very outside ring, careful not to be recognized. He glanced up to see a couple of kerosene lanterns now crash into the front of the building. The dry wood-framed store burst into flames and began to crackle.

He had just inched his way within twenty feet of El Viento and Creek, when she separated the group with a moon shot of the Greener. She rushed toward the front door, yelling above the noise at the men with drawn guns who were waiting for Brannon to flee the building with the prisoners.

"Stop it!" she screamed. "Don't you see? He won't come out! He'll never surrender prisoners to the likes of you!"

"Now, Miss Rose . . ." Highsmith reached out and grabbed her shoulder.

223

Her shotgun whipped around catching High-smith in the chin, splitting his lip. She shoved the barrel right against his bloody face.

"Don't you 'Miss Rose' me! You're trying to burn up the only God-fearing man left in this town!"

The men backed off, and she leaped for the door. She broke it open with the butt of the shotgun and stumbled inside. Black waves of smoke rolled out the doorway.

Brannon tried to scream above the crowd, but it was useless. He didn't even attempt to keep concealed now, but shoved his way violently through the melee. The men by the front door were so startled to see him there on the outside that they didn't bother raising their guns as he bulled his way through.

Brannon yanked his bandana around his mouth and sliced his way into the smoke-filled room.

"Miss Rose!" he tried to scream, but the words seemed muffled. "Rose?"

Overpowered by smoke, he lost sight of the room, the floor, even his hand with the Winchester. He started coughing. Then he stepped on something that caused him to twist his ankle. Reaching down, he felt the barrel of the Greener on the floor. Then on hands and knees, he began a frantic search for Creek.

He found her sprawled on the floor. He tried to pick her up, but he discovered his left arm had no strength at all due to the gash he had received earlier in the week. Instead, he draped her over his right shoulder like a sack of corn, reversed his footing, and pushed his way through the smoke.

Breaking out into the fresh air of a Rocky Mountain night, he ignored the command given at gunpoint to stop. The crowd gave way, and he crossed the street and laid Creek down on the wooden sidewalk near El Viento.

"Rose!" he wheezed.

The crowd pushed tight against them.

"Raise up her head!" he commanded a man standing right next to her. Then he put the palm of his left hand on her stomach and banged his right fist into the back of that hand repeatedly.

Come on, Rose. Come on!

She began to cough. Brannon, on his knees beside her, propped her up against his legs and chest. He held her shoulders and pulled her hair back out of her face as she struggled for each breath.

"Brannon," one of the councilmen shouted, "where are those prisoners?"

The question was ignored.

"I said, where are those prisoners?" the man repeated waving his handgun in Brannon's face.

The movement was so swift, the man was stunned. Brannon grabbed the right wrist that held the .44 and twisted it back in a crushing grip that forced the gun to drop to the sidewalk. The man dropped to his knees in pain.

"Mister, you set fire to the only tolerable building in this place knowing that I kept those prisoners shackled to a post! Attempting to burn men alive is a heinous crime!"

"They're still in there?"

"I can tell you this," Brannon snarled, "there's no one alive in there now!"

It finally dawned on some of the crowd that the fire could spread to other structures, and a bucket brigade was haphazardly formed to try to contain the flames. Others, who sobered up enough to realize what they had done, scattered back into the darkness.

There was still a mass of onlookers around Brannon and Creek as she started to come to. She remembered a burning building . . . and smoke, lots of smoke. And then there was Stuart Brannon.

Brannon! You pig-headed, self-righteous, stubborn fool! Don't you go and die on me trying to defend a couple of murderers!

She gasped for fresh air, coughed violently, and then became dizzy. Now she was coughing again. She heard someone call her name. Someone was holding her shoulders. Someone was stroking her hair.

Stuart? Strong arms and a tender touch. That's the way I had you figured. Brannon, you're easy to read.

People stared at her . . . a fire crackled . . . men shouted. Her right hand went to her chest as she tried to assist her lungs to pull in some fresh air.

"Stuart!" she gasped. "You . . . you're . . ."

"I made it out before the fire started."

"And the prisoners?"

He held his finger to his mouth to quiet her. "You just get to breathing proper. Is everything else all right?"

"I've got a pain in my stomach," she reported between gasps for breath, "but I'll survive. I don't know how you got out."

"The angels delivered me." She could tell he tried to smile, but it came out flat.

He bent down close to her ear. "When you feel up to it, I'll mount you on El Viento, and we'll see if we can slip out of this place."

She looked down at her dress, now soot-sprinkled and smeared.

"Brannon, since meeting you last week, I've ruined every dress I own, except the —"

"Buckskin? There's a seamstress in Tres Casas that could suit you up proper. Are you going with us?"

"Us?" she questioned.

Is this part of his plan? Brannon, just when I figure you've lost control, you tell me it's all a plan?

A princess in any tribe or culture, he thought as he helped her to her feet. *It's in her eyes, her manner, her authority. It's God-given. Every man's dream, but one man's tornado.*

"Mr. Brannon!" a voice cried out above the roar of the crowd and flames. "Mr. Brannon! They jumped me and got away!"

227

He turned to see a couple of men helping Jeremiah Gilmore limp through the crowd.

"Jeremy!" Brannon ran to his side. "What happened?"

"I did just like you said, Mr. Brannon, honest! But Rutherford was acting sick. I thought it might be a heart attack or something, so I goes to check on him and Cleve trips me up."

Gilmore clutched his side. Brannon could see blood seeping through his fingers.

"The next thing I know Rutherford pulled my gun. I tried to roll out of the way like I seen you do. The first bullet missed, but he clipped me in the side with the second."

"Rutherford ain't in Fetterson's?" one of the men shouted.

"He's still free?"

"Brannon set them loose, did he?"

"Jeremiah, where did they go?"

"Rutherford lashed out in Mr. Miller's wagon down that west road." Gilmore was breathing hard, and his eyes began to blur. Brannon was surprised to see Creek had found a tea towel from someplace and was holding it tight against Gilmore's side.

"How about Cleve?"

"Rutherford left him standing there. I saw him run off into the trees, but I don't rightly know where he ended up. I hurried to find you! I'm sorry I let you down, Mr. Brannon!"

"Jeremiah, there's no need for apologies. You stand a full sixteen hands, which is more than

I can say for any other man left in Paradise Meadow."

Word of the escape rippled through the town. Many firefighters dropped their buckets to get a more detailed report.

Brannon pulled a leather pouch out of his saddle bags and handed it to Creek.

"Rose, help Jeremy get that wound patched up. Then go immediately and buy the best team and wagon in Paradise Meadow. Load up your school supplies, Jeremy, and anything else you want to bring, and put that wagon out on that western road. We're going to get him to Tres Casas as soon as possible!"

"You're going after them?" she pressed.

"Yep. Me and three quarters of the citizens of Paradise Meadow." He motioned at the crowd surging around them.

He pulled himself up into the saddle and jerked back on the reins. El Viento reared up on his hind legs. The crowd on the ground jumped out of the horse's way, and Brannon spurred the big black gelding into the Colorado night.

TWELVE

Stuart Brannon had doubts that El Viento would ever make much of a cow pony. But there was no question that the big black gelding was the fastest, smoothest horse Brannon had ever owned. And El Viento ran best at night.

Dark shadows of tents, buildings, and then trees streaked by Brannon and disappeared into the night. He pulled up only for a moment at the clearing on the far side of the hanging log where Gilmore had held the prisoners. In the dark, there was no trace of their departure.

Rutherford had to take that wagon down this road! He can't unhitch the team and ride one of the horses because the shackles are still on his feet. But he won't stay on the main road. He'll pull off and blaze a new road if he has to.

Brannon knew that the vigilantes from Paradise Meadow were only moments behind him. He wanted to find Rutherford before they did. It was personal.

It was my error. I should never have put that young man in that bind. It doesn't seem fair for him to carry that bullet! Pull him through, Lord.

In daylight pursuit is easy. There would be wagon tracks, high visibility, and little opportunity for Rutherford to hide something as large as Miller's photographic wagon.

But it was not daylight.

Not even moonlight.

Brannon slowed El Viento so that he might carefully check every possibility of a turnoff.

When he gets lower down the mountain, those arroyos and barrancas will provide cover for two hundred miles! He could make it to Utah before I find him. Well, he won't take the fork back to Brighton Pass. And I doubt if he'll head down towards the Arizona line. But somewhere there's a trail back to the canyons. Red Shirt knew the way!

Suddenly he jerked the reins so hard that El Viento skidded to a stop. Brannon slid up to the horn.

"That a boy!" He patted the horse's neck. "Let's go back there and look!"

About fifty feet up the mountain, Brannon found the resemblance of a wagon trail winding through the trees. Scooping up a small pine branch covered with dry needles, he lit the needles. They flared up for a moment, revealing fresh wagon tracks headed down the trail.

Brannon walked El Viento for a while, following the tracks until the pine torch died out.

"Well, boy, I don't know how far he is, or if he's waiting for us in these trees!" he mumbled.

He remounted his horse and leaned low in the saddle with his sternum on the horn. His face bounced in the mane as he peered between the horse's ears.

"No reason to give him an easy target," he

whispered to El Viento.

Even though the night was dark, with only stars providing light, he could see the black shadows of the tall trees break away in the sky and reveal what had to be a wagon trail below.

After several minutes of this style of tracking, Brannon dismounted and struck a match, again finding the fresh wagon tracks. Just as the match faded back into darkness, he noticed El Viento cock his head and point his ears straight forward.

"What is it, boy?" he murmured.

Standing perfectly still, Brannon could hear the wind whip through the treetops. Then there was the eerie whine of a dead tree as it screeched and moaned while being supported by a live one.

He was just about to remount when he heard a distant sound of a hammer banging away on metal.

The shackles! He's trying to bust the shackles!

Continuing on foot, he led El Viento as quietly as possible. He kept stopping to readjust his direction toward the sound of the hammering.

I've got to get there before he busts out and mounts one of those horses!

Brannon hoped that Rutherford felt so secure and hidden that he had built a fire or dug out one of Miller's lanterns. That would provide a beacon to guide him to the fugitive. But, strain as he would, he could see no light at all and could only guess the route by the sporadic sound of hammering.

The night sky revealed an opening in the trees

ahead. Brannon knew he was coming to a small meadow.

This wouldn't be a bad spot. Pull across the clearing and park in the far trees. That way you could at least hear anyone approaching . . . maybe even see them!

Brannon didn't enter the clearing. He began a slow and deliberate walk through the woods to the right.

Stopping.

Listening.

Beginning again.

At first the sound grew more distant, but as he swung around the bottom edge of the clearing, he could tell it was getting closer. He could still see nothing and was forced to stop every three steps to listen. Finally the hammering stopped. So did Brannon. After a moment, there were several more hammer blows. Brannon again stepped forward.

Suddenly he heard a horse whinny not more than fifty feet in front of him. He froze and grabbed El Viento's muzzle to keep him from revealing their position. A small, round red glow about head high gleamed straight ahead of him.

A cigar?

Then he saw the glow fall to the ground.

He's going for his gun!

Brannon dove straight forward, pushing El Viento to the side just as a bullet tore through the night. A flaming barrel revealed the man's position. Brannon raised to fire at the target and then at the last moment failed to squeeze his finger.

How do I know for sure it's Rutherford?

He rolled behind the trunk of a tree, and one more shot blasted in his direction. He waited without making another sound.

Brannon figured it was only a couple minutes, but it seemed like an hour as each man waited for the other to move.

Lying flat on the ground, Brannon tossed a branch in the opposite direction and shouted, "Dixon, it's me!"

A shot rang out. Then Brannon heard a rough, startled voice, "Cleve? Is that you, Cleve? How in the —"

From his ground position Brannon caught a glimpse of Rutherford's outstretched gun hand silhouetted against the night sky. Using his Colt so he wouldn't have to raise up off the ground, Brannon fired two shots at the shadowy arm.

A scream, a crash, and a curse shattered the windblown stillness of the night.

"Cleve! I'll —"

"You're yelling at the wrong man, Rutherford. I didn't say it was Cleve. I said it was me." Brannon stayed low.

"Brannon?"

"Back away from that gun, Dixon."

Suddenly wild shots pierced the night.

Hoping to avoid a ricochet, Brannon waited for the guns to empty. With the clicking of empty chambers he heard movement.

He's trying to get back on the wagon and make a run for it.

Brannon, with Winchester in his right hand and Colt in his left, ran toward the sounds. He reached the back of the wagon just as Rutherford slapped the leather to the team. The wagon jolted and jerked its way into the night. Brannon tossed his Winchester into the rear of the wagon, grabbed the tailgate, and ran along behind.

Finally gaining a step, he leaped for the back of the wagon and pulled himself inside. Plunging toward the front, he found that the photographer's storage and dark room had only a rear entrance. He couldn't get to Rutherford. Stumbling over Hawthorne Miller's cooking gear, Brannon hoisted an iron bar used to hold pots over the fire.

Leaning over the back of the wagon, he jammed the bar into the spokes of the left rear wheel and jumped from the wagon. The wheel locked up. Several spokes snapped like toothpicks, and the horses yanked to the left. The wagon pitched onto its side, tumbling Rutherford out in front of Brannon.

He sprang towards the downed fugitive, but as he closed in, he saw an axe in Rutherford's right hand. Brannon couldn't avoid contact, but he protected his head with his hands and ducked at the same time.

Rutherford's panicked swing missed its mark, but the handle of the axe slammed into Brannon's left arm. He could feel the old knife wound tear open. Brannon lost grip on the Colt, but immediately he squeezed off one round from the Winchester into the dark.

He heard a thump. He waited several moments for any sign of movement, then lit a match.

The rifle bullet had punctured Rutherford below the chin, snapped his head back, and exited behind his right ear.

Rutherford was dead on impact.

Brannon rolled to his knees and grabbed his bleeding arm. Pulling off his bandana, he wrapped the wound the best he could.

He looked down at Rutherford.

"If I'd shot you a week ago, it sure would have saved everyone a lot of anguish!" he muttered.

They want Rutherford . . . they can come get him — and the wagon!

He lit another match and found a cloth of some sort in the back of the overturned wagon. Holding one end in his teeth, he managed to tie a crude bandage around his reopened wound. Gathering up his hat and his guns, Brannon hiked back up the wagon trail to find El Viento.

Unlike his previous horse, Sage, El Viento was not calm under fire. In fact, the horse had bolted up the mountain at Rutherford's first shot. If the big black, Mama Grande's gift to him, had any redeeming feature, it was that he always ran away the same direction he had come. Brannon knew El Viento would be somewhere up the trail towards the main western road out of Paradise Meadow.

The more scared, the further he goes! Maybe I should sell him and buy a cayuse that will stand and fight.

A half-hour later he could tell he was getting close to where the trail forked with the road. Then he heard hoofbeats of several horses and distant voices.

The vigilantes? Highsmith? It couldn't be Rose. She's supposed to be in a wagon.

Approaching the riders quietly, Brannon sneaked in close enough to hear their conversation.

"My word, it's El Viento! Brannon's down!"

"Which trail did you say this . . ."

Fletcher? Mulroney? Who else?

"I should have never let him take on a whole town!"

"I'd say the town is paying a bit itself."

"Well, don't put flowers on my grave yet," he called. Fletcher nearly jumped out of his saddle.

"Brannon? Good heavens, you could cause a man to have heart failure!" Fletcher blurted.

"Doc?" Brannon grabbed El Viento's reins as he talked. "Doc, what are you doing with this pair?" He pulled himself into the saddle, leaving his left arm limp.

"Vel sent me along. She insisted that if you rode back into Paradise Meadow, there would be lots of folks needing medical attention," Doc

Shepherd of Tres Casas responded.

"She's right about that. Got a knife wound in my arm that just busted open again."

"Tell us, Stuart," Fletcher quizzed, "what are you doing out here on the road without your horse?"

"Yes," Mulroney added, "and why is the sky lit up in the direction of Paradise Meadow?"

Brannon looked east. Even over the pine-covered crest, he could see a red-orange glow in the dark sky.

"Stuart, I did bring along my bag. I should look at that arm," Doc Shepherd suggested.

"They're burning the town down." Brannon sighed.

"Who's burning it down?" Fletcher asked.

"Everyone! They set Fetterson's on fire and tried to burn me out."

"Fetterson's? Burn you out? Why?" Mulroney groaned.

"A lynch mob was after Rutherford and Cleve. I was holding them prisoner until the U.S. Marshal gets here."

"He isn't coming," Fletcher announced.

"Why?"

"Cheyenne trouble on the eastern slope. They won't have a man this way until June at the earliest."

"Well, it's too late now anyway." Brannon shrugged.

"Why were you out here?" Fletcher pressed again.

"Chasing Rutherford."

"Did you get him?"

"Yep."

"Where's Miss Rose?" Mulroney quizzed.

"She should be rolling down this road in a wagon with Gilmore. He got shot up pretty bad trying to help me guard Rutherford."

"Do you want me to dress that wound now?" Doc Shepherd asked.

"After you look at Gilmore. We'll need to find them. You can tend to me later."

The owner of the livery stable was busy on the bucket brigade, but Creek found that talk of hard money for a team and wagon quickly caught his attention.

Brannon never asked me if I knew how to drive a team! He assumes I want to leave Paradise Meadow now. He assumes I'm willing to help Jeremy. He assumes I'll throw my belongings in a box and trail him down to a New Mexico town I've never seen.

Well . . . well . . . he's right!

And that's exactly what makes me so mad!

The man who sold her the wagon and team helped her load Jeremiah Gilmore into the back.

"Miss Rose," Jeremy spoke slowly and softly. "Miss Rose, do you ever pray?"

She tried to make him comfortable by wrapping him in an old quilt. "Of course, Jeremy. Everyone has prayed sometime in their life."

"Well, I don't pray much," he admitted. "But

239

tonight I prayed I wouldn't die until I reached Mr. Brannon. I guess my prayers were answered."

"I believe they were. Now, Jeremy, it won't be a very smooth ride, but we must get you to a doctor."

"Do you think Mr. Brannon ever prays?" he asked.

"Why do you ask that?"

"He don't seem like he ever needs God's help." Gilmore grimaced as he tried to move to a more comfortable position. "Why pray if you don't need help?"

"Well, you just might be surprised about Mr. Brannon. Some folks pray just to get help. Others, like Brannon, talk to God just the way a person consults his father."

"Guess it depends on how well you know the Almighty," Gilmore mumbled.

Rose Creek felt uneasy about the direction of the conversation. "Now I'm going to drive this rig over and pick up some of my supplies. Then we have to get on the road toward Tres Casas."

"Yes, ma'am." Just as she was about to sit down on the bench, he spoke again. "Miss Rose?"

"Yes?"

"Am I going to die?"

"I certainly don't think so. Why do you ask?"

"Well, if I'm cashin' in, I was thinkin' maybe I ought to settle things up with the Almighty."

"Jeremiah . . . whether you live or die, it would be good for you to settle things up. Don't you agree?"

240

"Yes, Miss Rose, I reckon you're right."

Physician, heal thyself! Who am I to lecture this young man about getting right with God?

After loading what was worth saving of her belongings, she turned the team away from town and circled the outskirts to avoid the burning buildings and those who'd remained to fight the fire. She noticed that most of the residents of Paradise Meadow just watched the fire from the front of their own tents or were packing up their belongings. She stopped and waited for one family to scurry in front of her. She recognized the small girl trailing her mother.

"Emilia?"

"Miss Rose? Are you leaving too?"

"Yes . . ." she stammered, "I . . . I need to get a wounded man to the doctor. Is your family moving on?"

"Yes, Miss Rose. Papa says this ain't no good place for children."

"Isn't . . . isn't a good place," Rose corrected. "Where are you going, Emilia?"

"Garnerville. Papa says everyone is getting rich up there. We're going to have a great big white house on a hill! Are you going to be our teacher in Garnerville, Miss Rose?"

"I don't think so, honey. But keep working hard for whoever might be the teacher. And keep practicing your penmanship. You have very lovely penmanship."

"Yes, Miss Rose, I will!"

Even in the fire-lit night the little girl's eyes

sparkled at Creek's sincere praise.

Lord . . . look I, eh, I know it's been a long time, but could You give this half-breed a place to teach and a classroom of children like Emilia? Please, Lord!

The fire from Fetterson's seemed to Rose to be spreading. The sky was so lit up it was almost like day. As she rolled along the edge of town to the start of the western road, several men stationed themselves by the hanging log. One man had crawled atop the log and was positioning two rope nooses.

It's time for the women and children to leave Paradise Meadow. They're going to find someone to hang tonight, no matter what!

"Jeremy," she called back, "we're at the west road now. How are you doing?"

"I hurt real bad, Miss Rose," he moaned.

"You hang on. Remember how you made up your mind to make it to Brannon? Well, I want you to work just as hard right now. Don't you go giving up on me!" she pleaded.

"No, ma'am, I won't. I'll hang on. You can count on me!"

She brushed away the tears from her eyes and slapped the leads. The wagon lurched into the night. As she crested the mountain behind Paradise Meadow, she stopped again to look back.

"Jeremiah? Do you need some water?"

"Yes, ma'am . . . I'm catawampously thirsty," he murmured.

Suddenly a dozen riders thundered straight at

242

her. She drove the team to the side to try to keep them from spooking.

Emerson Highsmith led the pack.

"Miss Rose? Are you leaving Paradise Meadow?" he called as the men halted and tried to settle their prancing, snorting horses. "I didn't think you'd ever quit!"

"Mr. Highsmith, I have been insulted, humiliated, and attacked. The school is destroyed and the only replacement building burnt to the ground. Now every family with any sense is leaving Paradise Meadow. I am not a quitter. This place has put off all semblance of civilization. That's a course I cannot reverse or tolerate."

"Is Brannon with you?" Highsmith asked.

"I thought he was with you!"

"Yeah, well . . . he hightailed it out of here, and we haven't seen him. Or Rutherford!"

"Miss Rose!" A pathetic holler came from a form strapped across the saddle of a horse. She rolled the wagon up to see Cleve, still in shackles, draped across the saddle like a sack of flour.

"Miss Rose!" he coughed. "You've got to get Brannon! They is going to hang me! I ain't never killed no one, no ma'am. Brannon knows! Get Brannon. Hurry, Miss Rose!"

"Even Mr. Brannon can't help you now!" she offered.

"He's the . . . he's the only one I can count on!" the man begged.

That's him — the man everyone counts on.

"Cleve," she replied, "you're going to have to

243

rely on a Higher Authority now."

"They're going to hang me, ain't they?"

"Every man's responsible for his own actions. Both you and they. You chose your own company."

"God have mercy on my soul!" he cried.

"Fortunately for all of us, His mercy is greater than our failures," she added.

"We don't need no lecture from a breed!" a man shouted. And almost at once the whole pack spurred on towards Paradise Meadow. She pulled the rildy up around Jeremiah Gilmore and drove the team on down the mountain. For some reason she could not explain, she began singing "Amazing Grace" in English and then in Cherokee at the top of her voice.

The words caught Brannon by surprise, but not the tune.

"I say," Fletcher called, "is that an Indian chant?"

"Sounds more like an old hymn," Brannon replied. The voice faded as they approached a wagon coming down the road from Paradise Meadow.

"Rose?" Brannon called.

"Stuart?"

He dismounted and walked over to the wagon.

"Was that Cherokee? I've never heard it before."

"It's been a long time for me, too," she said.

"Miss Rose, are you all right?" Peter Mulroney approached the wagon.

"Why, yes, Mr. Mulroney." She nodded. "And the children? Where are they?"

"They're safe in Tres Casas with Velvet, Mr. Brannon's friend," he reported. "But they miss you."

"Velvet?" she questioned.

"Oh, excuse me, Rose," Brannon apologized. "Dr. Shepherd, this is Rose Creek. Velvet is married to Doctor Shepherd."

"Married? Well, I . . . you're a doctor? . . . oh, Jeremy! He needs immediate attention!"

Brannon unlashed the doctor's bag from his horse and handed it to the physician as he hurried to the wagon.

"We've got to have some light," Shepherd called out.

"Peter, build a fire by the side of the road there."

"Speaking of fire, what's happening in Paradise Meadow?" Fletcher, the only one still on horseback, called out.

"I think they'll let it burn to the ground just to have a hanging." Rose sighed. Then turning to Brannon, she exclaimed, "Stuart, you're hurt!"

"Same old wound."

"You found Rutherford?"

"Yeah."

"Is he . . ."

"Dead."

"I passed Highsmith and vigilantes back up the road. They had Cleve hogtied and were headed for a hanging. He begged me to find you so that you could stop them!"

Brannon ran his hand across his face to the back of his neck and sighed.

"I can't stop them," he admitted. "A week ago we stopped them. But now they'll do it no matter what. It's like a taste of poison."

"I know . . . I just wish . . ."

"Peter, help the doc with some light. Rose, you pitch in too. Fletcher and I will ride up to town. Maybe an outbreak of common sense will strike the region."

"I'm coming with you," she insisted.

"No, Rose. Look, there are some things a woman shouldn't have to see. I'm asking you, don't ride with us."

She stared at Brannon for a moment and then nodded agreement.

Brannon and Fletcher galloped up the trail.

The scene at the hanging log struck Brannon as bizarre. A nightmare.

"It's Dante's inferno!" Fletcher gasped.

In the background tents and buildings burned, some unchecked. At others the owners desperately tried to extinguish the flames.

Around the hanging log itself, several dozen men sat horseback. Another twenty or so were scattered about on the ground, staring silently as the firelight flickered off the lifeless body hanging from a rope.

Brannon rode past the riders without looking at them. None of them offered any resistance.

He untied the end of the rope and lowered Cleve's body to the ground.

Then he turned El Viento towards the vigilantes.

"Which of you men would like to make ten hard dollars?"

"I would!" a man on the ground spoke up.

Brannon tossed a coin at him through the shadows. "You know where that little clearing is on the other side of the creek by the aspens?"

"Yes, sir."

"You take him over there tonight and bury him. Bury him deep, you hear?"

"Yes, sir, I'll do it." The man and another toted Cleve's body off into the night.

"Now look, Marshal —" Highsmith began.

"Don't 'Marshal' me," Brannon shouted. "I am not the marshal of Paradise Meadow! Not now, not ever. Not for one minute, not for one day. I don't want anyone to ever say I was marshal of this town. There was no law when I rode into this place . . . and there is no law now!"

He dismounted and threw his rope over one end of the hanging log. Everyone watched as he latched the rope used as a noose around the same end of the log.

Remounting, he tied his rope to the horn of the saddle. "Edwin, dally that noose rope!"

Side by side, they walked the horses to take the slack out of the ropes. Then they spurred the horses, and on the third try the hanging log crashed to the ground.

Brannon turned El Viento back towards the west road and recoiled his rope as he rode along.

No one said a word.

Brannon never looked back.

Fletcher kept silent as they loped their horses up over the mountain and down towards the others. Brannon wouldn't have heard him even if he had spoken. He was tied up with another conversation.

Lord, I can't do anything with people like that. I can't change 'em, I can't control 'em. I can't even contain them. Maybe Rose was right. Maybe I've been trusting just in my own strength.

But not here.

Not any more.

I didn't make Paradise Meadow a better place to live. In fact, if anything, it's worse.

It's Yours.

Forgive 'em if You must.

Change 'em if You can.

Save 'em if You want.

Lord, folks down here on earth are a far cry from perfect, but we could've done better than this!

When they reached the others, they found camp had been made in a break in the trees just off the wagon road. A campfire crackled and a coffeepot hung over the flames. Doc Shepherd was wrapping up Jeremy's waist while he sat propped against a couple of saddles. Bedrolls were scattered around the fire, and Peter Mulroney and Rose Creek were in deep conversation.

"Did they . . ." Creek questioned the men as they rode in.

Fletcher nodded.

Brannon pulled off his saddle, blanket and bridle and hobbled El Viento near the other horses. Then he walked back to the campfire.

Rose Creek stumbled for words, then blurted out, "Stuart, you'll never guess what Doctor Shepherd told me. Oh, by the way, why didn't you tell me he was mayor of Tres Casas? Anyway, the schoolteacher there just quit to get married, which I was telling Peter was an insufficient reason for abandoning one's post, and Mayor Shepherd asked if I would like the position!"

As if suddenly awake from a dream, he stopped and stared at Creek. He tried to remember what she had just said.

"Eh, that sounds great, Rose . . . teach in Tres Casas? You can stay at Vel's hotel. How about you, Peter?"

"Well, Mr. Boswick asked me to make the Little Yellowjacket run for him, at least until he mends. Why, he even talked about allowing me to buy in. The children would be delighted to have Miss Rose for a teacher, so I'm leaning towards Tres Casas myself."

"Wishy! I forgot about him! Is he all right?" Brannon asked.

Doc Shepherd rejoined the others and answered the question. "Wishy is going to pull through fine. He had a concussion and will carry a permanent crease above his ear, but he should get

249

his balance back in a few days."

Brannon poured himself a cup of coffee and sat down next to Shepherd.

"Doc, I think you better look at this arm. It was healing fine until I ran into that axe handle tonight." He glanced at Creek. "With your permission, Rose, I'll pull off my shirt and let the doctor bandage this wound."

"Certainly." She nodded, sipping on a tin cup filled with coffee. "I suppose you two will be going to Arizona now?"

"First I have a promise to keep. To get those twins out of my hair, I told them to wait in Tres Casas, and I'd buy them supper. So, I suppose I'd better."

"The twins!" Fletcher shot straight up. "My word, Brannon, I forgot to tell you."

"Did they get murdered? Arrested?"

"Quite the contrary!" Fletcher reported. "They bathed, washed, and combed their hair — for the first time in months, I'm sure — and purchased new clothing. After that, they boarded the stage to San Francisco."

"The twins in San Francisco? Is this some sort of British joke?"

"I'm serious. They took passage to San Francisco!" Fletcher insisted.

"Where did they get the funds for that?" Brannon quizzed.

"Well, actually . . . I . . . you know what a nuisance they were . . . and —"

"And you shipped them off to a lion's den

like San Francisco?"

Rose smiled as she gazed at the fire. "Don't worry about Deedra and Darrlyn. They can take care of themselves wherever they are."

"They chose the destination," Fletcher added. "But they did mention telling you the dinner offer still holds if you ever come to San Francisco."

Brannon looked over at Fletcher. "I'll certainly keep that in mind! In that case, Edwin, we might as well start down that trail to Arizona tomorrow."

"My word," Fletcher pondered, "you don't suppose Red Shirt and friends are still waiting for us?"

"It all depends on whether they got hungry or not," Brannon mused.

"Arizona!" Doc Shepherd tied off the bandage on Brannon's arm. "Vel gave me a letter to deliver to you, and I almost forgot. It came to the hotel right after the wedding, but we didn't have a way to get it to you."

Brannon started. "A letter?"

"Yes." Shepherd looked at the name on the outside. "All I know is that it's from a Miss Harriet Reed in Prescott and that when I mentioned that name, Vel raised her eyebrows and repeated a rather uppity, 'Oh, her!'"

"Miss Reed?" Fletcher smiled. "Now this could be quite interesting. You will read it aloud, won't you, Stuart?"

"Miss Reed? What is it with Brannon? Does he have ladies waiting in every town?" Creek jibed.

251

"There's another letter inside this letter!" Brannon called. "It's from the Indian Territory."

"Not from Fem Sem, I hope," Creek put in.

"Read them one at a time. Surely you don't have any secrets from us, do you?" Fletcher needled.

Brannon scooted closer to the flames and held the letter down so he could read it in the firelight.

Dear Mr. Brannon,

This letter of yours came to my attention, and I held it for a few weeks awaiting your arrival. Hearing recently that you wintered in Tres Casas, I took the liberty to forward it on to you since it was marked "urgent."

On a personal note, we have found a delightful home on a hill behind the courthouse. You are cordially invited (by my sister and her husband) to dine with us the next time you travel through Prescott.

Sincerely, Miss Harriet Reed

"By my sister and her husband," Creek mimicked. "Sure. She could have been more subtle. It's obvious she's out to grab you, Stuart."

He looked up with a blank stare. "Miss Reed? Oh, no, not her. She's not that type."

"We're all that type," Creek chided. "If the right man comes along."

He opened up the letter marked I.T.

"Fletcher! This is from Elizabeth!" Brannon shouted.

"Really? Can she write?"

"Listen . . . listen."

Dear Mr. Stuart Brannon
  of Arizona Territory,

How are you? I am not good. Mrs. Quincy writes these words for me. Littlefoot and I were with Chief Joseph at Bearpaw. The army captured us and brought us here, but this is not a good place to live. Many have become sick and died.

They will not let us return to our homes in Oregon and Idaho. But I was told if someone would write a letter promising me a job and send money for the trip, then they will let me leave. You are the only one who can help me and my brave warrior. I can cook and clean on your big ranch in Arizona. You know I will work hard. And Littlefoot is no burden.

Please write to me quickly. I am afraid of the sickness.

Your very good friend,
Elizabeth

"Brannon," Fletcher broke in, "what will you do now?"

"Send her the money and offer a job." Brannon shrugged.

"But you aren't sure what's left at the ranch."

"Edwin . . ." Brannon paused, then continued, "I'll tell you what I am sure of. I'm sure Miss Rose is going to make one excellent teacher. I'm sure that Sean, Sarah, and Stephen are going to finally get settled into a stable situation. I'm sure that Edwin Fletcher has not heard the last of the Lazzard twins. I am sure that Stuart Brannon is going to retire from public life and spend the rest of his days doctoring sick cows, breakin' frolicky horses, and watching sunsets. And I am most certainly sure that I can find Elizabeth steady employment in Arizona. She's got a consuming desire to see that little one raised up right . . . and I think she deserves a chance."

Creek walked over and sat down next to Brannon. "Which tribe is Elizabeth?"

"Nez Perce . . . but it's a long story."

"I've got time." She took a stick and stirred the fire.

"Well, if this gets too dull, you certainly have my permission to go to sleep," Brannon added.

For the next three hours Rose Creek didn't even doze.